Love Letters to Michigan

Christine M. Lasek

This is a work of fiction. Names, characters, places, and incidents either are the product of the author's imagination or are used fictitiously, and any resemblance to actual persons, living or dead, business establishments, events, or locales is entirely coincidental.

ELJ Publications, LLC ~ New York
ELJ Editions

Library of Congress Control Number: 2016946288
ISBN 13: 978-1-942004-24-0

A NOTE FROM THE AUTHOR

There are a few people I would like to thank, without whom this book wouldn't have been possible.

Andy, Brian, Leigh, Macklin, Peter, and Seth—thank you for writing the letters that helped get me into my MFA program.

John, Karen, Katie, and especially Ira and Rita—thank you for your guidance, support, and your infinite patience.

To all my USF MFA peeps—thank you for sharing in my heartaches as well as this success.

Jim—for helping me be in the right place at the right time and supporting me every step of the way.

To my family, especially Tom, Diane, Amanda, Angela, and Dan—thank you for your love and support. It sustained me.

And to my dearest Ryan—I couldn't have taken this journey without you. We did it!

CONTENTS

Misspent Youth   3

Growing Up Healthy   23

The Makeshift Carrier   45

Sisters   61

I Don't Belong Here   79

Orderly   101

The Disenchanted Youth   123

Misspent Youth

Even with the bedroom door closed, I could hear the mantel clock marking the seconds—a monstrous art nouveau piece cast in bronze and featuring a woman holding her hat to her head against a gust of wind no one else could feel. It was an extravagant Christmas gift purchased from an antique dealer, a last-ditch effort by a lover who knew he was on his way out. All that happened twenty years ago, the passage of time smoothing any residual wistfulness—but if I sold the clock or gave it away, there would be a hole on my mantel, the absence of the clock as intrusive as the item itself.

There were a lot of seconds between 4 and 8 a.m. I tried to count them, but I could feel myself becoming drowsy. Reading and watching television had the same effect, and I refused, at 4 a.m., to log onto the computer in order to check email or do work. Besides, receiving an email from their professor at that time would only reinforce my students' belief that I had nothing better to do with my life than deny their requests for extensions or refuse to bend on my attendance policy.

So I sat—first in the yellow glow of my nightstand lamp, then in the cool light of the early morning sun leaking around the shade, until the red digital numbers on my clock shone 7:59.

"Pryce Funeral Home. How may I help you?"

Even over the phone, Garrett Pryce's voice is unmistakable—thick and languid, pairing perfectly with his dark set, heavy lidded eyes, his oversized hands.

"This is Callie Forsythe."

I hesitated—what had seemed like a great idea in the dark at 4 a.m. now felt ephemeral, like smoke in sunlight.

"Is my mother still in your morgue?" I asked.

Garrett was silent a moment, and I could almost hear him thinking of how to respond. But I couldn't help him. I couldn't tell him about my recurring dream that my mother was still alive, that today's viewing and tomorrow's service were mistakes that I not only would have to explain to Mother, but to the legions of mourners on their way to Ridgevalley from all over Michigan, not to mention Chicago, Atlanta, and Portland.

"Everything is set for today's viewing," he finally responded.

"And her body is there?"

"Yes, your mother's body is here."

"You're sure?"

"I saw her myself not fifteen minutes ago."

Garrett was good—he said "her," not "it." Very sensitive.

"Thank you. I will see you in about an hour."

"If there is anything else you need before then, please do not hesitate to call."

I was both embarrassed and relieved when I hung up the phone. Since I wasn't sure which I felt more, I considered it a wash. Besides, I doubted this was the strangest conversation Garrett had ever had with a bereaved.

I'd finally gone to sleep at midnight the night before, but woke two hours later, a vivid dream still tangible, like an echo or the thick sweetness on your tongue long after the wine is swallowed. In the dream, my landline rang—it was Mother, the day after she was supposedly buried in the ground.

"You idiot girl! I'm not dead," she said and coughed wetly. "You have to call the family and fix this. And on your way over, stop at the drugstore. I need my inhaler."

My eyes popped open—wide-awake, heart pounding. Not because I was afraid of my mother, but because I was having a hard time deciding where the dream ended and reality began. That uncertainty bred panic.

I took a few deep breaths, told myself that Mother had just died and dreams of this sort were to be expected. But when I dropped back to sleep, I fell right back into the dream, as if it had continued playing during my brief period of wakefulness.

I was walking up the path to my mother's home in Hudson, not the Holy Name Hospice Center where she'd spent the last month of her life. The lawn was lush and green, the dogwood shading the front steps was in bloom—I could see the veins of pink blushing the white blossoms. A white pharmacy bag crinkled and bulged in my hand, overstuffed with Mother's prescription inhaler and a pack of her beloved Bel Air cigarettes.

I fished around my pants pocket, looking for my keys. The door opened before I found them, but I woke up before the door opened all the way, certain that Mother was still alive. It was then I decided to just stay awake until the funeral home opened at eight.

§

After the overwhelming outpouring of love and support from the family, much of which I hadn't seen since Uncle Al died and everyone flew out to Portland for the funeral two years ago, my godson's companionable quiet was a welcome reprieve.

"I know your dad's worried about me, but you didn't have to stay," I called to the kitchen from the couch.

I wasn't sure what Jeremy was doing in there. After the funeral, after the luncheon in the basement of the church, the family ascended on my house to eat, drink, and reminisce. Before leaving, my cousins had washed and put away all the dishes, found places for the covered casseroles in the refrigerator, wiped down the counters, and swept the kitchen floor.

Jeremy emerged with a mug of peppermint tea and plate of chocolate crinkle cookies. He kept his dark hair longish and had a habit of brushing the heavy locks out of his eyes. When he took a seat in the leather club chair next to the couch, he hung his gangly legs over the arm.

"It was my idea to stay, Aunt Callie, not my dad's."

Jeremy's dad, my cousin Derek, and I grew up like brother and sister. Before he and his wife left the house after the funeral, Derek had shed his suit coat, tie, and dress shirt so he could mow my lawn. I refused to let him prune my neglected hedge.

"I bet your mother loved that." I sipped the tea. Jeremy had let it steep for the perfect amount of time—the peppermint was pronounced, but with no residual bitterness.

"You're too hard on her." Jeremy helped himself to one of the cookies. When he bit into it, a dusting of powdered sugar snowed into his lap. He tried to brush it away, but it only left smears of white against the black wool. "You forget that she lost her mother years ago. She knows what you're going through."

"That doesn't mean she's happy to share you."

Jeremy shrugged, stuffed another cookie into his mouth.

Derek and I were closest while I was getting my Ph.D. at the University of Illinois. He and Dana were newlyweds, living thirty minutes away in Monticello, a dinky starter home with one bathroom and dingy-white aluminum siding. In between teaching composition to freshman and exploring the boundaries of the Southern Gothic genre, I would entertain Derek and Dana during Friday bar jaunts in Champaign, or we would cook Sunday night dinner together in their dark kitchen.

While Dana was in the hospital having Jeremy, I took time away from rereading Eudora Welty's complete works in preparation for my comprehensives in order to clean the house top to bottom and prepare chicken potato casserole and wild rice turkey bake, dishes whose recipes promised they froze beautifully. Derek had asked me to be Jeremy's godmother—a job I took seriously.

But the arrangement lost its charm for Dana when I moved back to Michigan for work and a six-hour drive rendered weekend visits impossible. I took to keeping Jeremy for a week every summer. He started taking the train alone at thirteen.

"How did you convince your school to let you take time off at the end of the year?" I asked. It was the middle of May, and Jer still had a month of school to go.

"My dad talked to the principal. Besides, it's better to take off a week at the end of the year than in the middle—most of the time left will be spent on reviewing ahead of end of the year exams."

"How's AP English?"

"I'm expecting an A."

"That's my boy!"

"You say that, but I hated Tennessee Williams."

"He's an acquired taste. You'll discover Eudora Welty in college and your life will never be the same."

I'd said it without thinking, but even without his mother there to tsk, the word 'college' thickened the air between us. Last Christmas, after the ham and eggnog but before the pumpkin pie, one of the cousins asked Jeremy about his plans for after graduation.

"I want to study mortuary sciences."

Derek, who'd been going around the room with a bottle of Bailey's Irish Cream, froze. "You mean you want to work with dead people?" he asked.

I watched Jeremy take a deep breath. "Yeah."

"We can discuss this later," Dana said, taking the bottle of Irish Cream from Derek's hand and continuing his circuit around the room. Her voice was light, but when she splashed a little of the booze into my glass, her eyes were glittery and dangerous.

Jeremy wafting the plate of cookies under my nose brought me back to the present. "Hey! Here's an idea! Why don't you eat one of these delicious cookies?" He helped himself to another before setting the plate down closer to me. "Aunt Sharon made them especially for you."

I narrowed my eyes at him. "I'm eating."

"Not during dinner you didn't. You pushed tuna casserole around your plate."

I wanted to tell him to not worry, but yawned instead.

"See? Cookie first, then bed."

"I didn't sleep very well last night."

Jeremy closed his mouth on whatever smart retort he was going to make and his face softened, the crinkled brow and pursed lips of pity. It was a very adult look on his seventeen-year-old face, and I found it disconcerting, so I picked up one of the cookies and put the whole thing in my mouth.

"Better?" I asked, spitting a cloud of powdered sugar.

"Much," and when he smiled, he was my child-like godson again.

§

That night, the dreams were different, but the feeling was the same—somehow, I had made a horrible mistake. Of course Mother wasn't dead, and how would I explain this to the family? But whatever the manifestation, I never saw my mother's face—it was obscured by menthol-flavored smoke, or behind a partially open door. She was only ever a voice, coming at me from up the basement stairs, or from the next room, or over the telephone. And after every manifestation, I awoke panicked, ten minutes later, or twenty, or an hour. And every time, I'd have to talk myself back into sleep.

I got out of bed at 8 a.m. feeling like I hadn't slept at all and pulled my dressing gown over my pajamas. I was frustrated, as always, when the satin tie refused to stay knotted.

When I peeked into Jeremy's room, I saw he was already up, the sheets and blanket pulled up over the pillow. My ranch, built in the sixties, is too much house fifty-one weeks a year, and Jeremy has his own room. The collection of toys and books kept therein is like a physical manifestation of Jeremy's growing, tree-rings comprised of die-cast models of Thomas the Tank Engine, plastic dinosaurs, Legos, and hand-constructed models of race cars. Each toy loved for the week of his visit and then left to wait patiently for Jeremy's return, not knowing that, a year later, Jeremy would be older, with different interests and changed tastes.

I poured myself a cup of the coffee Jeremy made and found him on the back porch, cup to his lips, watching the willow tree leaves wave silver and green in the morning light.

"You're up early," I said, closing the sliding glass door carefully to keep from sloshing my over-full mug.

"Hardly. I've been getting up at 5:30 all year. This is a break."

I took the only other patio chair, the metal cool through my pajamas and robe, and sipped my coffee. The grass was perfectly cut, even around the willow tree's gigantic trunk. When did Derek have the time to edge?

"So what do you want to do with the time you're here?"

A few years ago, when Derek suggested that I spent too much money during Jer's visits, I told him truthfully that, had it not been for my one week a year, I would never leave Ridgevalley. During his visits, Jeremy and I hit the Detroit Zoo, the big library downtown, or the art museum. Two years ago, Jeremy wanted to spend time on the beach—so I canceled my summer classes and rented a cabin on the west side of the state. We spent that week cooking outdoors, hiking Sleeping Bear Dunes, and swimming in chilly Lake Michigan.

"You know, the Belle Isle Conservancy reopened the aquarium," I offered. "You haven't seen it in years, and you used to love it there.

It might be fun to go back."

"I'm here for you, Aunt Callie. Is there anything you need or want to do?"

"No, my darling. I am just glad you're here."

He blushed—it wasn't that long ago that Jeremy'd allow me to gather him in my arms and read to him from his favorite books— *Alice's Adventures in Wonderland, Peter Pan,* and *Little Lord Fauntleroy.* One week a year really wasn't enough. The long, pale fingers encircling his coffee mug, the pensive set to his mouth, might as well have belonged to a stranger.

"Well, if you wouldn't mind, I'd like to check out Wayne State while I'm here."

The surge of elation was like a million tiny butterflies fluttering up my esophagus. Wayne State was only an hour and a half away. He could live with me and commute.

"It's the only school in Michigan with a mortuary science program and one of only a few programs affiliated with a big university."

"What did your folks say when you told them you wanted to check out funeral schools in Michigan?"

"I'll let you know when I tell them." He got up from the patio and walked out into the yard. It wasn't very large, a characteristic common to neighborhoods built during that time period.

"Do you know my mom told me that I didn't really want to study mortuary sciences? According to her, I'm just 'being morbid'?"

"That's probably not the best way to go about discussing it."

"No."

I drained the rest of my coffee and put my cup down. "If it makes you feel any better, my mother didn't understand my career path, either."

"Being a college professor?"

"Well, going to graduate school, anyway. My mother was born in

1938. She thought I should get married and have children, like the girls I went to high school with. Or, if I insisted on going to school, I should learn something useful like typing, so I could get a job as a secretary."

Jeremy made a face. "I'm trying to picture you as a secretary—it's not working."

"It was the eighties—don't forget my shoulder pads, perm, and Diet Coke."

"Did she come around?"

I didn't want to tell Jeremy, No—she never forgave me for not marrying early and having children, for not choosing the life she couldn't have when my father abandoned her, thirty years old and pregnant.

"Of course. Your mom will, too." I felt bad lying, but unlike my mother, I was certain Derek would help Dana come around. "At the end of the day, mothers just want their children to be happy. And if you're happy putting makeup on dead people, she will be, too."

Jeremy circled the willow tree, delicately trailing his fingers through the hanging branches like strands of a beaded curtain. Even from my seat on the patio I could see his face pinched with worry. Once he made a full circuit, he paused and smiled. "Maybe that's how I should put it to her. 'I just want to put makeup on dead people. Is that so hard to understand?'"

"Good plan." I rose and stretched. "I'll get dressed and we can head downtown."

As I collected our coffee mugs, Jeremy said, "For breakfast I had one of the muffins from the basket your colleagues sent. They're all individually wrapped, so it wasn't stale at all."

"Is this going to be the theme of your visit? 'Hound Aunt Callie until she eats everything in sight'?"

He shrugged.

"How about I take you to lunch after our campus visit? There's a great restaurant close to Wayne's campus that serves dim sum. You can sit across from me and watch me inelegantly stuff steamed barbecue pork buns in my mouth, okay?"

§

Tian was a small restaurant on the edge of Wayne State's campus. The dark interior was a strange mix of Asian opulence and industrial sparseness—the black table between Jeremy and I featured a red, gold, and green dragon, incongruous with the building's exposed ceiling beams and duct work.

The crowd was equally eclectic. Students and local shop owners wore dangling earrings, printed scarves, hooded sweatshirts and Converse—a bright contrast to the gray and black suits of the business people that populated the high rises of Detroit's New Center area.

"I'm sorry we didn't get to see much of the college," I said, shedding my coat and taking a seat.

"Are you kidding? It was great!" Jeremy said. He hadn't spoken much as we poked around the building, but his eyes were enormous, taking in everything. When he opened his menu, however, his smile turned quizzical. "So, uh. What's good here?"

"During lunch and dinner, you don't order off the menu."

Our waitress appeared then, diminutive, her jet hair pulled back in a knot at the base of her neck. She carried two sweating glasses of water and Jeremy's bubble tea—the black tapioca pearls like giant fish eggs in an iced tea sea—on a cork-lined tray.

"Ready to order?" she asked.

"We'll just order from the cart." I handed the menus to her.

"The cart?" Jeremy asked, and as if on cue, a woman appeared from between the swinging doors separating the dining room from the kitchen. She was pushing what looked like a stainless steel airline beverage cart with steam rising from it. Unlike our waitress and the hostess, the girl pushing the cart was not Asian, her blond dreadlocks tied back from her face with a scarf.

"Dim sum?" she asked when she got to our table.

"Please," I said. Jeremy raised an eyebrow at me as the woman rattled off the offerings. I selected shrimp kau and parsley and scallop kau, pink and green showing through the almost-translucent dumpling wrappers. I also chose steamed barbecue pork buns, sticky rice in lotus leaves, egg tarts, but passed on the tripe and chicken feet. When the woman rolled her cart away, the dragon on our table was completely hidden by stainless-steel steamer containers.

"Where have you brought me, Aunt Callie?" Jeremy asked, pulling apart his wooden chopsticks and pouring soy sauce into a little black and red glazed dish.

I picked up one of the scallop dumplings, dipped it in Jeremy's soy sauce, and put the whole thing in my mouth.

"I'm eating," I said, enunciating around the dumpling.

"I can see that."

"So, tell me about this program," I said while Jeremy stabbed at the doughy barbecue pork bun with his chopsticks. "We didn't really see much at the school, and what we were able to see looked like the city morgue in every police procedural crime show."

"That was the embalming laboratory! I've researched the program online. It's comprehensive. I'll take classes on everything from small business management, to anatomy, and grief counseling."

I shook my head. "And this is really what you want to do?" I thought of mother's funeral, memories stinging sharply, but recalled with the hazy recollection of something that happened years, not hours, ago. At one point during the viewing, I stepped outside to get some air, and I saw Jeremy in Garrett Forsythe's office. They were speaking animatedly to one another. I'd meant to ask Jer about that conversation later, but forgot.

"Yes." Jeremy said this with the finality of someone digging in his heels in preparation for a long argument.

"It just seems—sad." I knew it sounded lame, but it was the best descriptor I had. Funerals were sad—for everyone. All the times I met with Garrett, he was always appropriately solemn.

"How am I supposed to eat this?" he asked, indicating the sticky rice.

"You cut open the leaf and eat the rice inside."

While involved with his lotus leaf, and without looking up, Jeremy said, "I just see death differently than other people, I think. I think it started when I was little, after Grandma died."

"You remember that? You were only four."

Dana's mother died suddenly of a brain aneurysm. "I don't remember her dying, necessarily. And I don't even remember her all that much—but I remember after. I know her death hit Mom hard. To cope, she used to go to the cemetery a lot—sometimes three or four times a week. And since I was home with her, she would take me with her."

"Your dad was okay with you going to the cemetery so much?"

"I don't know that Dad knew. But don't look so weirded out! It wasn't as big of a deal, at least to me, as it sounds. Sometimes Mom talked, like Grandma was there. Sometimes she just sat. But she rarely cried, which I think is the only thing I would have found scary or disconcerting. We would go a lot, then less often, until we were only going on holidays and Grandma's birthday in March. To be honest, it wasn't until Grandma Ann died that I thought about those visits at all."

He was talking about Derek's mother, who died of Hodgkin's Disease three years before. Unlike Mother, Aunt Ann hadn't spent any intermediary time in a hospice facility. According to Derek, she never even woke up during her final days in the hospital.

I had driven to Ludington for the funeral, a freak early-November storm blowing snow diagonally across the road. The four-hour drive was almost doubled, my chicken casserole going stone cold within its insulated carrier.

"My dad was just about incapacitated with grief, you know?" Jeremy continued. "And my mom, too. And I was sad, of course. But not completely undone. No crying jags, anyway, and I think my calm was a comfort to them both. I liked it—feeling like I was helping."

"So why not be a psychologist?"

"Because I like the other parts, too. The science of the body, the art of the reconstruction. Sorry, Aunt Callie. Sad or not, I am bent on being a funeral home director some day."

I thought about Mother—she refused to attend my graduation from University of Illinois. She'd claimed, at the time, that it was too far to travel, even though Derek had offered to drive her out and bring her home again. I knew the real reason she wouldn't come was because she was mad. It was evidenced in the snide remarks about me being "married to my work," in the incessant questions of "Are you seeing anyone?" and "Are you intent on being an old maid?" While she was in hospice, lung cancer metastasizing to her bones and her brain, morphine taking her in and out of lucidity, she turned to me once, her eyes perfectly clear, and said dryly, "I am going to die before meeting my grandchildren."

"Well, I think being a funeral home director is going to be great," I said.

"Yeah?"

"Yes. I feel like I'm still figuring out what I want to be when I grow up. Somehow, at seventeen, you already know."

§

When Jeremy set the table for dinner, he put my plate at one end of the wooden table that seats twelve and his at the other. In between, there were Pyrex baking dishes of turkey tetrazzini and tuna noodle casserole. There were white Rubbermaid containers of broccoli salad, ambrosia salad, and fruit salad. There was a plate of brownies covered in cling wrap, tins of cookies, a white waxed box with squares of homemade fudge.

"Who is going to eat all this?" I asked. After our time downtown, I'd napped all afternoon. My dreams were quiet, preferring, I think, to steal in under the cover of darkness.

"Me," Jeremy said. He spooned tuna noodle casserole and popped his plate into the microwave. "I liked the dim sum a lot, but it wasn't very filling."

"Are the dishes labeled with who brought what?" I inspected the tin of cookies. Penguins were ice skating around the perimeter. There was no label. "I am going to have to send thank you notes."

"You shouldn't be worrying about that. Turkey tetrazzini or tuna noodle?"

"Turkey." Once the microwave dinged, Jeremy replaced his dish with mine.

He heaped the other half of his plate with equal parts broccoli salad and ambrosia salad and commenced eating. "This stuff's kind of strange," he said, pointing to the pink lump of ambrosia. "There's marshmallows in it."

He took my plate from the microwave when it dinged and, without asking, heaped it in the same manner as his own plate.

"Yeah, dishes like that were more popular when I was growing up. Ambrosia salad was one of my favorites."

I thought of family cookouts, of Derek and I running through sprinklers at Aunt Ann and Uncle Harry's house, water droplets sparkling in the sun like a slow-motion commercial for life insurance. Aunt Ann and my mother would wear matching flower-printed aprons over their cotton dresses, my mother's ever-present cigarette trailing ghosts in her wake. The memory was as sudden and violent as a pin prick, bringing tears to my eyes before I could swallow the first fluffy bite.

If Jeremy saw my sudden emotion, he didn't acknowledge it, focusing instead on his plate, on working systematically through his food of grief.

"I noticed the willow tree in back isn't looking too good," Jeremy said, after I had dabbed my eyes with my napkin and resumed my eating.

"The city's wanted to take it out for years. Now that it's sick, they're going to get the chance. The tree company is actually coming on the day you fly back."

"Why does the city care what kind of trees you have in your backyard?"

"Willow trees have strong, far-reaching roots that can muck up water pipes and sewer systems. You're not allowed to plant any new ones, but Ridgevalley can't technically make me get rid of it, since it was here before the new law. That doesn't stop them from sending me a yearly letter announcing 'free removal of troublesome tree species.'"

"I'll be sorry to see it go."

"Me, too."

"My dad called while you were asleep. He gave me a list of chores that he didn't get a chance to complete while he was here."

"I don't want you to spend your last day here doing work."

"I like to help, Aunt Callie. And except for mowing, which my dad already did, I like yard work. Then before heading to the airport, I'd like to go to the cemetery to see Aunt Sarah."

The thought of going to the cemetery was cold and sick-making, a lump of phlegm in my chest threatening to crawl up my throat, a ball of emotion sitting hotly in the bags under my eyes. I suspected Jeremy's wanting to go visit the cemetery again so soon had less to do with him than with his desire to fix me. Like the food he consistently urged on me, a trip to the cemetery would, in some way, sustain me like a not-stale muffin. But after our conversation that afternoon, about Jeremy's childhood trips to the cemetery and the role he saw himself playing in the family's griefs, I didn't know how to ask him if this were the case. His dark eyes, the inscrutable set of his jaw, belonged more to a stranger than to my nephew.

§

That night the dream was different. No accusations of burying her too early. No talking at all. It was just Mother, sitting in her favorite chair, her package of cigarettes on the armrest. A lit cigarette sat smoldering in the ashtray—a long-ago souvenir from Bablo Island in the shape of a ship's wheel.

I stood between Mother and the television, the table lamp bathing her in a thick yellow glow.

Mother's mouth was a line, lips grooved like stitches from years of smoking. Her once Lucille-Ball-red hair was a wispy white cloud on top of her head. Her eyes, as clear and certain as they'd ever been, bore into me, forced on me all of her disapproval and disappointment.

I could feel it, like a too-warm blanket. Like the rasp of second-hand smoke in the back of my throat. Like the pressure of unshed tears.

The dream, a purgatory of motionless tension, lasted forever. When I finally awoke, my consciousness was a long time in coming, a slow swimming to the surface, mouth dry and eyes gummy with sleep.

§

Jeremy picked ineffectually at the dirt beneath his fingernails as we drove to the cemetery.

"I wish you'd have let me run and get you a pair of gardening gloves," I said. He'd spent the morning weeding flower beds and trimming the hedges around the front of the house. When he tried my gloves, he couldn't even squeeze his hand through the lavender, elasticized opening. But he wouldn't let me help in any way, insisting that I sit in the shade on the porch, drinking coffee and eating muffins that, despite their wrappings, had begun to go stale.

"Eh, you might have been right. I have two lovely calluses from your pruning shears. A couple of thick branches refused to be pruned."

"Now you see why I let it go so long."

"You sleep better last night?"

I glanced at Jeremy, then back at the road. "How do you mean?"

"Well, I didn't hear you thrashing around in your sleep is all."

"I wasn't aware I was disturbing you."

"You weren't, Aunt Callie. And you weren't talking or anything—I could just hear you moving around, but not last night. Last night, you were quiet as the dead."

"Clever," I said. I drove through the gates of White Chapel Cemetery. It was a newer non-denominational cemetery, and from the road, the inset marble headstones were invisible, the whole thing looking like some strange golf course surrounded by an austere metal fence.

"I hope I remember where we have to go."

"I remember," Jeremy said, his voice quiet.

The road was winding and paved with bright white stones that crunched under my Camry's tires as I crawled along. The dogwood trees scattered throughout were still saplings, too small to cast any meaningful shade, but still blooming in the cool May afternoon.

"Stop here," Jeremy said. He jumped from the car before I even put it in park and charged across the lawn. He walked parallel with the headstones, turning invisible corners, so as not to walk over the deceased. I wondered if it was a habit he developed when frequenting the cemetery with his mother. Maybe it was just professional courtesy.

I stood and waited, car off and driver-side door open. To continue down the road if Jeremy was wrong. To make a quicker getaway.

"She's here," Jeremy called, and I closed the door and followed him. Mother's plot looked just like the others—mottled grey marble headstone—except that the grass over her grave was light, newer. Other than that, it looked like it had always been there, and I found this disconcerting.

I hung back while Jeremy knelt to pay his respects. The sun shining off his bent head teased red and gold highlights from his dark hair. His lips were moving, but I couldn't hear what he was saying.

He crossed himself and stood, and I waited for him to encourage me to pay my respects in a similar way. I didn't know how to tell him that I didn't have anything to mumble over the grave as he had.

But instead, he just brushed off his knees. "Ready to leave?"

§

Before he could disappear into the terminal, I hugged Jeremy fiercely and made him promise he would at least talk to his dad about having visited Wayne State.

"I'll make you a deal," he said, pulling out of my embrace and shouldering his backpack. "I'll promise to talk to my dad if you promise to eat something tonight."

"I don't know if I can face the turkey tetrazzini without you."

"The tuna, then."

I hugged him once more, my arms not fitting all the way around him and his backpack. I promised him I would eat.

Which is why, on the way home, I hit the McDonald's drive-thru, the thick smell of a Big Mac and fries filling the car in a palpable way. When I pulled into my driveway, my house looked dark and unfeeling. I didn't think I could face the quiet, the wide expanse of my empty kitchen table, so I turned off the ignition and ate my meal in the front seat. I chewed and swallowed in a deliberate, utilitarian way, and tried to remember the last time I indulged in fast food. I couldn't remember. When I wiped my hands on my pants, it left satisfying grease marks sparkled with salt.

I decided to spend the last few moments of daylight on the back porch. But when I walked around the side of the house, I was shocked to see the bright white stump in the place where my willow tree once stood. It was smaller than I thought it would be, vulnerable and exposed in the waning light.

All of my emotions suddenly felt huge, like a hot air balloon filling impossibly fast inside of my body and threatening to carry me off. Luckily, my dinner sat like a brick in my stomach, mooring me in place.

Growing Up Healthy

Salon Mani-fique was always tropically warm, and even in the mild spring weather, condensation crawled up the windows. Jason liked to run his fingers through it, tracing patterns with jagged edges, where the water droplets coalesced, grew heavy, then plunged to the floor.

"Don't do that," his mother said, tugging his foot to the floor, so that he sat with his back to the window. "It leaves streaks. The Chinese ladies don't want to clean it." Jason's mother said she went to the "Chinese ladies" for her acrylics because they did the best work for the price.

"Why's it so warm in here?"

"Probably to keep people from getting sick. Everyone's sitting around with their hands or feet in water."

Jason nodded but thought his mother was wrong. Near the cream-colored pleather couch where they waited was a huge palm in a heavy red and gold pot. If Jason sat too close to the end of the couch, the branches poked fingers into his neck and ear every time the front door opened. He thought the heat was for the plant, which had dried ends and yellowed fronds. There was a similar plant at his dentist's office, which was always too cold, but that plant was bright green and plastic.

"Why don't you read your book until it's time?" his mother asked.

Jason's book was a dog-eared paperback of *Superfudge*, NORRIS ELEMENTARY SCHOOL stamped smearily across the cover. Last year, the entire fourth grade class had read *Tales of a Fourth Grade Nothing*. Jason wasn't enjoying the second book in the series nearly as much. He understood Peter in the first book—Fudge was a total pain. But Jason couldn't relate to Fudge's reaction to his new baby sister—not least of all because, now that his mom and dad were divorced, Jason would never get to have a baby sister of his own.

"It makes my hands smell weird," he said.

"The book does?"

"Yeah. I think it's old or something."

The title page was spotted with mildew. Someone had scrawled Pen15 in pencil, and someone else had gone in and tried to erase it, but the defacement was still clearly visible.

"Besides, I'm almost done with it."

"What will you read next?"

"A book called *Hatchet*."

"Sounds exciting."

Jason shrugged. "I'll let you know."

"You get pedicure today?"

The nail tech's face was framed by her black chin-length hair. Her black dress was printed with daisies, and there was a small daisy embroidered on the string tied around her delicate neck.

"I'll only have time for a fill today," Jason's mother said. She reached up and patted where her silver-streaked hair was swept into a banana clip.

"Hana almost finish." She turned to Jason. "Ready?"

Jason nodded and rose to his feet.

"If you finish before I do, just come find me around the wall," his mother said. "And don't forget this."

Jason took *Superfudge* from his mother's hand, and watched as she sniffed her fingers and wrinkled her nose.

"Told you," he said, and followed the nail tech into the long room lined with pedicure chairs—the same cream-colored pleather as the waiting room furniture, nestled atop white ceramic basins.

This would be Jason's fifth pedicure and he considered himself an expert, but he still felt self-conscious as he removed his shoes and socks. There were two women also getting pedicures, jeans rolled up to their knees, feet hidden inside the foot basins. They stopped their conversation when he entered the room.

"Ooh. Fancy shoes," the nail tech said. Jason's black LA Gear high tops were new and had red lights set in the heel that flashed when he walked.

"They were a birthday present from my dad," Jason said, shoving his balled-up sweat socks into them.

§

When Jason overheard his mother describe the acrylic nails to his Aunt Susan over the phone, his mother called them "a necessary luxury." Jason's mother was a compulsive nail-biter, nibbling her fingernails down past the tops of her fingers, the jagged edges biting into the soft skin they were meant to protect. The typing she did as a receptionist for an insurance company made her fingertips bleed.

"I left streaks of blood on the keyboard and the cleaning crew flipped," Jason's mother explained to her sister. "My boss said I'd have to wear band-aids to work if I didn't stop biting them. There's no biting them, now. I'd break a tooth."

Jason thought the nails looked like talons, shiny and red, sometimes set with crystals or striped with gold foil. The first month she wore the fake nails, Jason's mother raked them through her son's mousy hair, or ran her index finger up along the knobs of his spine, giving him goosebumps. When she tapped her fingers on the tabletop during dinner, she smiled at the sound—the rat-a-tatting of tiny hammers.

Every other Thursday, after she picked Jason up from school, the two of them went to Salon Mani-fique, so the nail techs could spackle over the new nail growth, file down the ends with dremel tools, their noses and mouths protected from the acrylic dust by seafoam green surgeons' masks. The air on the manicure side of the salon hung heavy and acrid, the smell of lacquer, of polish removers, and the cloying scent of strawberry hand lotion warred with the acrylic dust for supremacy.

At first, Jason hated these trips. His mother made him sit in the waiting area until she was finished. She would say, "Since you're waiting, get a head start on your homework," or, "Read your book." But usually, Jason spent the hour watching people arrive for their appointments, watching huge white and gold koi swim around the tank behind the front desk, or flipping through gossip magazines—the faces of celebrities rippled with moisture. One time, one of the ladies behind the desk offered him some orange juice that came in a can with a pull tab, but the juice tasted funny, a metallic tang that sat on his tongue, and Jason declined a drink every time one was offered after.

Then one day, while Jason's mother was waiting for Hana to call her back, an older woman with lines around her eyes and the sparkle of silver in her hair led a much younger nail tech into the waiting room and offered a "discount pedicure" to Jason.

"This Mi Sun," the older woman said. Mi Sun nodded her head and smiled. Jason thought she had a pretty face and liked that her front teeth were crooked. "She new. She practice pedicure at discount?"

"Oh, well, that's a very nice offer, but I don't know that I'll have time for a pedicure today," Jason's mother replied.

"On little boy during your fill?" the older woman asked.

Jason looked at his mother, whose eyes had gotten very wide.

"Do men usually get pedicures?" his mother asked.

"Oh yes," the woman replied. "Is different, just soak and buff and trim nails. No polish for boys. Mi Sun is new, but good student, and I watch."

Jason's mother opened her mouth to reply, but then closed it, shrugged, and turned to him. "It's your feet they're talking about. Do you want a pedicure?"

"What is it?" Jason asked. At Salon Mani-fique, Jason had only seen the waiting room, the station where Hana filled his mother's nails, and the bathroom.

"It's pleasant. You soak your feet in warm water and this young lady will make sure you have no rough skin on your heels and your toenails are trimmed," his mother explained.

"Does it hurt?" Jason asked, heat rising to his face, painfully aware that the older woman and Mi Sun were listening to his conversation.

"Not at all. You're almost eleven years old—it's up to you."

Jason thought about the hour before him—he could start his math homework, an adding decimals worksheet, or he could read about Kelly and Dylan's affair on *90210* in the latest issue of *Teen Beat*. He glanced at the fish tank, but the koi hung motionless that day.

He took a deep breath. "I'll do it."

"You follow Mi Sun," the older woman said as Jason got to his feet. He glanced back at his mother once, who smiled, mouthed "Go on," and picked up a magazine.

The rows of pedicure chairs were empty. Mi Sun wheeled a tiny stool in front of one and started filling the ceramic foot basin with water.

"Take off shoes please," she said, her voice quiet against the rushing water splashing into the basin.

It had snowed that morning, a heavy, late-February snow that seeps through regular tennis shoes, so Jason was wearing his Spiderman boots, which were almost too small for his feet, the graying insulation hanging like a wisp of storm cloud from a tear in the plastic along the sole.

As Jason teetered on his left foot, yanking at his right boot, he watched as Mi Sun scooped some rocks from a jar and dumped them into the water, instantly turning it blue.

"What's that stuff?" he asked.

"Special salt," the older woman replied, appearing from around the wall. She held out a hand and helped Jason scramble into the pedicure chair. He was one of the shortest boys in his class and had to sit on the edge of the chair to dangle his feet into the water.

It was hot, but not uncomfortably so, and blue like the aquarium exhibits he saw during a field trip to the Toledo Zoo. His feet were obscured in the jetting water, but when his wiggling toes breached the surface, they looked to Jason like little fish hunting for food.

"Temperature good?" the older woman asked, and Jason nodded. She reached over and pressed a button on the armrest, which caused the chair to start vibrating.

Jason found the first part of the pedicure uncomfortable—Mi Sun's fingers were gentle, but the fact that she was touching his bare feet made him feel shy. When she used the file on his heels, it tickled so much it was everything Jason could do to keep from squirming and laughing. Mi Sun also tried to talk to him, asking him about school and his family, but her accent was so thick that he had a hard time understanding her, and he was too embarrassed to tell her so.

But soon, Mi Sun got to work on his toes, smoothing away the cuticles and trimming and filing the nails, which didn't tickle at all. She also stopped talking to him and spoke, instead, to the older woman, who was sitting in a nearby pedicure chair, watching. Even though Jason had no idea what they were talking about, the conversation was pleasant to hear—lilting intonations, the ease of familiarity. He wondered if Mi Sun and the older woman were related, and if so, how.

When Jason and his mother drove home, she asked how he liked the pedicure.

He thought for a moment. "I liked it a lot. At the end they use a lotion that smells minty and makes your feet tingle, and it's better than sitting and waiting on that couch."

"Good," his mother said. "It was pretty inexpensive. And with your toenails trimmed, it will cut down on the number of your gym socks I have to darn."

"Darn?"

"Sew holes closed."

"You sew my socks?"

"Sometimes," his mother replied, sticking her tongue out at him. "Or I replace them."

§

Jason never had another pedicure with Mi Sun. He still saw her sometimes—working the front desk, or with the bottom half of her face covered with one of the manicure facemasks. She always smiled at him, but he didn't know if it was out of recognition or politeness. He hoped that she remembered him.

"Water good?" the nail tech with the chin-length hair asked. Jason nodded, watched the water bloom blue with the scoop of salts.

Once the nail tech got to work with the file, Jason leaned back in the chair, his shoulders, neck, and head resting where the small of his back would have been if he'd been taller. The vibrating chair made it impossible for him to read his book—the words blurry on the page. Jason didn't understand why the chair vibrated, but it never occurred to him to ask, and ladies getting pedicures seemed to like it—they would lean their heads back, close their eyes, the slack skin on their faces blurring like the words in his books.

And Jason found, when he leaned back and closed his eyes, too, that the nail techs would chatter amongst each other instead of trying to talk to him, which was one of the things he liked best about the entire process.

Sometimes, he took their intonations and translated the conversations in his head. His nail tech with the flower-printed dress seemed upset about something, her sentences ending in long a's and ah's, and there was an air of impatience. Her companion, working on one of the jean clad women a few chairs over, spoke in the soothing tones of understanding.

Jason imagined that his nail tech saw *Superfudge* clutched in his hand, and was relating to her friend about how much she hated that book when she read it in school. He then imagined that the nail tech was talking about his LA Gear high tops and how she wished she had a pair just like them, but in silver with hot pink trim. Jason was sure she wasn't talking about Dylan and Kelly's stupid affair on *90210*.

§

Once Jason was finished with his pedicure, he walked around the wall and saw Hana ringing up his mother. Hana looked to be about his mother's age—but where fine lines were starting to crackle the skin around his mother's eyes, Hana's skin was perfectly smooth. She wore her black hair in a loose bun at the nape of her neck.

"You tell your mother to stop biting nail," Hana said, typing his mother's credit card number into the reader. Her punching, like her tone, was impatient.

When his mother was pensive, when she went over the bills at the kitchen table in the evening or watched the news, the nail on her ring finger would drift slowly, almost imperceptibly, down her face. Jason would watch as she took the nail delicately between her teeth and bit down. This was different from the frantic chewing she did before getting acrylic nails. This was controlled, one consistent bite that wouldn't let up, and caused a perfectly-spherical moon crater in the polish on that finger.

"What color'd you get?" Jason asked.

His mother displayed a red that was slightly lighter than the red she had before.

"Spring is coming," she said. "I thought a lighter color would be festive."

§

When Jason and his mother climbed into the powder-blue Ford Tempo, which had been parked in full sun, they both shed their coats to soak in the warmth.

When his mother fired up the car, the four members of ABBA started urging Jason to take a chance on them. The radio in the Tempo hadn't worked since before his father left, but the tape player still played, and permanently housed a cassette of ABBA's *Gold Album*.

Sometimes his mother rolled down her window and had Jason roll down his, and they drove down the highway with "Dancing Queen" blaring desperately over the rushing wind. Other times, his mother switched off the player and they drove in silence.

"You know, Mom, I have that tape in my backpack that Mike gave me for my birthday last week. We could listen to it."

Jason grabbed his backpack from off the back seat, rooted around until he found the cassette, *He's the DJ, I'm the Rapper*, under his math book. There was already a crack in the case's plastic, further separating the Fresh Prince from DJ Jazzy Jeff.

Jason ejected ABBA and fed his tape into the slot, which fired up in the middle of "Parents Just Don't Understand."

Jason already knew most of the words and mouthed along with the Fresh Prince. When he hung out at his friend Mike's after school or on the weekend, they sat on the floor in his room, where Mike kept the boombox he got for Christmas. Hyped-up on Coke, cheese and pepperoni Bagel Bites burning the roofs of their mouths, they listened to whatever cassettes Mike found in his older brother Brian's room: Marky Mark and the Funky Bunch, LL Cool J, Motley Crue. Jason liked The Fresh Prince and DJ Jazzy Jeff the best—even when The Fresh Prince was rapping about being in trouble, it still seemed like he was having a good time.

When the song was finished, his mother lowered the volume so she could talk over the start of "Pump Up The Bass."

"You like this?" his mother asked.

Jason studied his mother's face—looking for criticism or disappointment. Mostly, she just seemed surprised.

"Well, yeah."

"Oh."

§

Jason and his mother sat at the table eating lunch, each with their favorite sandwich—Jason's a Goober peanut butter with the grape jelly stripe on white bread, his mother's a bologna and American cheese on white bread. They both had piles of shoestring potatoes from the yellow and red canister in the middle of the table and a translucent smear of grease was growing out from under the edges of the crispy sticks on Jason's paper plate.

Jason's mother put down one of her sandwich quarters, chewed what was in her mouth and swallowed, and started to scrape at a milky white ring on the table's surface where Jason had left a sweating glass of orange juice for too long. His mother's talons scooped the imperfection away in neat rows.

"Do you like this lunch?" she finally asked, her water-ring task half finished.

"This is my favorite lunch," Jason said. And it was. He liked it best when the Goober jar was brand new—lines of grape jelly forming a perfect star in a sea of peanut butter. It was like cutting into an apple in just the right way and seeing something beautiful that most people just ate around, then discarded.

"It's just, I talked to your dad yesterday."

Now it was Jason's turn to put down his half-eaten sandwich quarter, chew what was left in his mouth and swallow. He folded his hands and waited, eyebrows raised in what he hoped was a curious-but-not-nervous way.

"He says I feed you too much junk food."

"It's a sandwich," Jason said. "You only let me eat ice cream for breakfast, like, three times a week."

His mother smiled—mission accomplished.

"Well, I might as well let you eat ice cream for breakfast. Lucky Charms?"

"They're magically delicious, Mom. I can't help it."

"Your dad told me that Amber made some kind of casserole thing with wheat berries and chickpeas that you really liked."

Amber was his father's girlfriend. She had short reddish-blond hair that curled and stuck to her forehead when the weather was hot. The cotton sundresses she wore, in brown or green or orange, showed tanned shoulders sprinkled with freckles. In the wintertime, she kept the sundresses, but covered her legs and arms with jeans and sweaters.

She liked to make casseroles out of things like butternut squash and kidney beans. When Jason's dad lived at home, the family's favorite dinner had been hamburger night—his mother cooking the hamburgers in a pan, toasting the buns with butter before piling on catsup, mustard, pickles, and lettuce.

Jason shrugged. Food was food—as long as no one was trying to get him to eat green peppers, he was generally happy. "It was okay. A little strange. Kinda chewy."

"But you liked it?"

He wasn't sure where his mother was going with this line of questioning. He was careful to not talk about his weekends with Dad and Amber too much—not that he thought his mother wanted to live with his father again. Jason just didn't want his mother to think HE was thinking of the three of them living together again.

"Well, you know, Amber made it," Jason finally said. "She wanted me to like it. And it wasn't gross or anything. I just don't want to eat wheat berries every day."

His mother nodded and resumed eating her sandwich. Satisfied that he had managed to avoid something uncomfortable, Jason put a pile of the shoestring potatoes in his mouth. Before he could finish chewing, his mother asked, "Do you always think about that? About how people might react to things you say and do?"

Jason looked at his mother, her sandwich suspended and her eyes glittering. There was something wrong, but he couldn't tell if she was angry or upset.

"I guess so," he said, spraying bits of half-chewed potatoes onto the table.

"You're a good boy," his mother finally said, but quietly, as if she wasn't sure that she meant it.

§

Jason's next pedicure was performed by the older woman who had watched and chatted with Mi Sun that first time. As she bent down to check the water temperature, the silver in her hair glinted in the halogen light.

"Water good," she told Jason as he eased his feet in. "I get tools."

While Jason waited, he heard the bell over the door announce a new customer, then the sounds of three women talking at once, asking for pedicures, comparing nail polish colors.

When the receptionist led the women around the partition, all three stopped chatting and stared at Jason, his dark blue corduroys rolled up to his knees, ankle deep in swirling blue water.

The women were young, Jason thought, not much older than high school girls. They were also all dressed alike, in tight black t-shirts with OPA CAFÉ! printed across the front in white. OPA

CAFÉ! was a diner in the same strip mall as Salon Mani-fique. The girls carried with them the heavy smells of fried potatoes, vegetable soup, and sweat.

In his hands, Jason clutched his library-bound copy of *Hatchet*, the next book in his class's reading series. He opened the book at a random page, pretending to read, hoping to discourage the women from continuing to stare or speak to him.

Three nail techs appeared from the back room, began filling foot basins and ushering the women into pedicure chairs. Once their feet were in water, they seemed to forget all about him, and continued talking—about their manager named Tony who was a jerk, a dish-washer named Romo who was cute, and the bitchy lady at table nine who always ordered fish, wore torn up nylons, and never left tips.

The older nail tech appeared from the back, her tools wrapped in a faded purple towel, and she got to work on Jason's feet.

"Ooh. Look," she said, lifting one foot from the blue water. "The toe has hair."

Jason had noticed that himself. Last year, the fourth grade class had been divided up into two groups—the girls stayed in the classroom with Mrs. Petrosky, while the boys were taken into the gymnasium with the gym teacher, Mr. Grayling.

All of the fourth grade boys in the school watched a video called *Growing Up Healthy*, which seemed almost entirely about body hair and nocturnal emissions.

After the host's prompt to stop the video, Mr. Grayling hitched up his gym shorts and asked the students if they had any questions. None of the boys raised their hands, and soon after, they were led back to class.

For the rest of the day, the girls sat huddled together, whispering. Every time Jason or one of the other boys looked at them or tried to listen, the girls stopped talking and started giggling.

Jason sat in front of Teresa Banks, one of the most obnoxious girls at Norris Elementary. "I already have MY dot at the end of the sentence," he heard her say to Emily King.

"What's that even mean?" Jason asked.

"That's enough chatter," Mrs. Petrosky said.

"Stop listening in, pervert," Teresa hissed. Jason sighed and went back to answering chapter eleven's social studies discussion questions.

"So what were the girls doing while we were watching our video?" Jason asked his mom that night. She knew he'd seen *Growing Up Healthy* that day, because she'd had to sign a permission slip. Jason had wanted to ask Mike about what the girls were giggling about, figuring his older brother Brian might have clued him in, but there hadn't been time before Mike's bus left and Jason's mom arrived to pick him up. "And what's 'dot at the end of the sentence' supposed to mean?"

"She was talking about her period," his mother said. "And from the sounds of it, she wasn't being very mature."

They were at the dinner table, and Jason was fishing the peas out of his tuna noodle casserole. Even though he didn't like the peas, his mother's tuna noodle casserole was his favorite—the one they served at school was too soupy and used elbow macaroni instead of bowtie pasta.

"No surprise there. Teresa sucks. So what's a period?"

"Girls go through puberty different from boys. Boys get all the stuff you saw in the video and girls start menstruating. Their breasts and hips get bigger, and when they're older, they'll be able to become mothers. But until then, one week out of every month, girls bleed from between their legs."

"What? Really?"

Jason's mother nodded.

"Like, a lot of blood?"

"Not a lot, but enough that they have to wear special pads to keep it from getting on their pants."

"It sounds gross, Mom."

"Grosser than peas?"

Jason knew his mother was trying to change the subject, and he was glad. "I'd eat this entire pile of peas if it meant I didn't have to watch *Growing Up Healthy* with Mr. Grayling again. It's bad enough when he's hurling a dodge ball at my head. I don't want to ask him about wet dreams!"

"Yeah, he is weird," Jason's mother admitted. She speared some of Jason's discarded peas with her fork and popped them into her mouth. "It's the shorts, I think."

"It's definitely the shorts! He even wears them outside in the winter!"

§

"Don't worry," the nail tech said, taking a pair of tweezers from off the cart. "I fix."

In the middle of trying not to yelp as the nail tech pulled the budding hairs from Jason's toes, the OPA CAFÉ! girl seated closest to him leaned over the chair arm and said, "Hey kid. You get pedicures often?" She had blond hair pulled into a ponytail. Her forehead was shiny and dotted with acne. Her smile was smirky, and for a moment, she reminded him of the girls in his class.

Jason realized this was not going to be one of his enjoyable pedicure experiences. The tops of his toes stung, and the OPA CAFÉ girls were so chatty that the pretty nail techs working on their feet remained silent.

"I get them sometimes," Jason said.

"I've just never seen a little boy get a pedicure before is all," the girl said. Her two companions snickered.

"Well, you're not seeing that now," Jason said. "I just had my birthday last month, and the second I turned eleven, I stopped being a little boy."

The girl's mouth fell open, shiny forehead wrinkled in confusion. It wasn't until Jason smiled and returned to his book that all three OPA CAFÉ! girls started laughing.

"You're okay, kid," blondie said and turned back to her friends. Talks of Romo resumed, and Jason was left in peace for the rest of his treatment.

§

Jason knew his parents were going to fight, despite his father's smile and talks of the Tigers' season tickets he had already bought for them. Jason could tell by the way his father gripped the steering wheel, the way the coppery-colored hairs on the back of his father's hands stood out so starkly against his pale skin. Jason could see the pending fight ticking in the corner of his father's eye.

"Next Sunday they'll be playing the White Sox," his father said. "That'll be a great game! I'll even spring for nachos, if you promise not to tell Amber when we get back."

Amber's latest creation, cream cheese and lentil casserole, sat heavily in Jason's stomach. He could feel his anxiety over the pending argument moving under it, like earthworms when a stone is disturbed.

When Jason's father parked his Jeep in the driveway, Jason could see his mother watching them from the front window, and knew that she knew a fight was coming, too.

Jason's mother's smile was wide and fragile when she opened the front door to let them in, lips stretched and quivering over her teeth. She was wearing her house clothes—a hunter green sweat suit, spotted with paint and bleach, worn only for cleaning. Her hair, pulled back in her banana clip, looked greasy.

"Did you have a good weekend?" she asked, pulling Jason into a hug.

"Hey, champ. Why don't you go upstairs and unpack your things so your mom and I can talk?"

Jason shouldered his backpack and trudged up the stairs, but instead of going into his room, he took his normal spot behind the wall at the top of the stairwell. He sat silently on the goldenrod carpeting, across from the upstairs bathroom, which was still bleachy from his mother's cleaning. He fingered the section of wallpaper where the glue had started to give, bubbling at the seams.

"We spent most of Saturday in the 24-hour clinic," his father said.

"What? Why? Why didn't you call me?" his mother said.

"He kept itching his feet. I thought at first it was some kind of athlete's foot, but then he told me that you've been taking him to some kind of Asian massage parlor for manicures? What the hell were you thinking, Helen?"

"It's not like that," his mother said.

"Don't you watch the news? Those places are filthy, filled with skin-eating bacteria."

"Is that what Jason has?"

"No. The doctor said the tops of his toes were irritated from having the hairs pulled out, and that's why he was itching, told me to pick up some hydrocortisone cream."

Silently, Jason removed his high tops, then his socks. The cream had helped the itching, but there were still little red dots on the tops of his toes from where the nail tech had yanked the hair.

"That's a relief," his mother said.

"You're missing the point, Helen. He's an eleven-year-old boy. He should be out playing basketball with his friends, not having the hairs pulled out of his feet by strangers."

His mother said nothing.

"You're making him weird. I had to root him out of a book so I could take him to the zoo today. That's not normal," his father said.

His mother said nothing.

"Look." Jason's father's tone was different. Less insistent and angry. Jason knew from listening to past fights that this was the beginning of the end, and he was thankful that it hadn't gone on for too long. "I know you're doing your best. But you have to think. What would his friends at school say if they knew about this manicure thing? It's bad enough he's got to split his time between homes—let's not make things any harder for him, okay?"

"Okay."

Jason heard his father leave, heard his mother bolt the front door behind him, heard his mother start up the stairs. Normally, he would have snuck into his room, closed the door silently, and pretended to be engrossed in something else—separating his laundry, finishing up his math worksheets—at this point in the fight.

But this time, he just sat and waited for his mother to discover him at the top of the stairs.

Instead of admonishing him for listening, she simply said, "Dairy Bar?" Jason nodded, pulled his socks back on.

§

It was a windows up, tape player off ride to the Dairy Bar—a frozen custard stand that opened April 1st and closed October 31st every year. The outdoor seating consisted of black-painted cement tables and chairs that were too cold in the spring and fall and scorching hot in the summer.

But it was a tradition—before Jason's mother and father split, and any time after there was a fight about him, he and his mother piled into the Tempo and drove to the Dairy Bar for custard. Jason always ordered the same thing—chocolate and vanilla swirled together and dipped in cherry, a bright red coating that hardened immediately, so he had to bite through the shell to get to the melting ice cream.

In mid-April, it was cool enough that he could eat his cone at a more leisurely pace, without the fear of vanilla and chocolate running down his arm.

His mother had a Reese's Pieces cyclone. As she fished the candy bits from the vanilla custard, they left behind brown, yellow and orange smears.

"I'm sorry I told Dad about the pedicures," Jason said finally.

"You shouldn't be," his mother said, her voice thick with custard. "It wasn't a secret. And I don't want you to feel like you have to keep stuff from your dad."

"But he got really mad."

"He got mad because he loves and worries about you. He used to get to see you every day—now he gets you every other weekend. It's not what we intended."

"He thinks I'm weird."

"You really shouldn't have been listening to us talk," his mother said. "Stuff gets said in the heat of the moment that wouldn't be said otherwise."

Jason licked all around his cone to catch any drips.

"And you're not weird—you're just different from him. He worries it's because of the divorce, but I don't think it is. I think you'd be different from him even if your dad and I were still together."

Jason's mother put her half-eaten cyclone down, placed her ring finger nail between her teeth and bit down.

"Did you tell Mike about the pedicures?" his mother asked.

"No way."

"How come?"

"He wouldn't get it."

His mother was silent while Jason began chomping into his cake cone.

"Well, I think we're going to have to stop the pedicures," his mother said.

"But it wasn't a fleshing eating bacteria."

"I didn't realize they were pulling the hairs out of your feet, though. I should have been paying closer attention."

"That only happened the last time. It was that older lady that did the pedicure, and she decided that the toe hairs needed to come out."

"Well, I've decided that the toe hairs need to stay in," his mother said. She gathered up her half-eaten dessert, wiped up a few ice cream drips from the table with a paper napkin, and threw them in the trash. Jason finished his cone, but his hands were sticky. He rinsed them in the ice-cold water fountain, the tissue-thin napkins disintegrating faster than he could dry his hands.

"We'll let your dad call the shots on this one," his mother said as they climbed into the Tempo.

"Okay."

Before she pulled out of the parking space, Jason's mother asked, "Hey. Do you have your rap tape on you?"

Jason pulled *He's the DJ, I'm The Rapper* from the pocket of his windbreaker.

"Play that parents don't understand song," his mother said, ejecting ABBA. "We'll dedicate it to your dad."

§

Years later, Jason thought about what he would have done differently, had he known the toe-hair pulling, OPA CAFÉ! girls session would be his last pedicure. He might have asked about the paraffin wax option on the menu board, or questioned why the chairs vibrated. He might have asked his nail tech's name—along with the names of all the nail techs.

But he never went back to Salon Mani-fique, and it wasn't long before his mother stopped going, too.

One day, when Jason got home from school, the smells of the nail salon hit him as he came through the front door—acetone and lacquer. His mother sat at the kitchen table, which was spread with newspaper and topped with cotton balls and little glass bottles of clear polish. Her talons were gone, and in their place were thin, brittle nails the color of wax paper.

"They're gone," Jason said. He dropped his backpack and sat in the chair across from his mother.

She shrugged. "The upkeep was expensive and a pain."

"What's all this you're doing?"

"I had the fake nails on for months," she explained. "My real nails underneath are like a baby's nails. I'll need to be careful of them for a while, until they're strong again.

"How was school?"

"I got an A on my *Hatchet* test," Jason said, pulling the much-crumpled test from his backpack.

"Good job! I don't think you ever told me about that one. Did you like it?"

"It was okay," Jason said. "It was about a boy that is the only survivor in a plane crash, and he has to live in the wilderness alone until he's rescued."

"I thought, with a name like *Hatchet*, the book would be exciting," his mother said.

"The hatchet was actually a present from the boy's mom," Jason explained. "She gave it to him right before he got on the plane. It was how he survived in the wilderness."

Jason watched his mother nod, half-listening, while she carefully painted another layer of clear polish on her baby nails. Eventually, she would go back to biting them, past the quick. She would develop a new way of typing to keep from bleeding all over her keyboard.

But Jason knew his mother's actions weren't in anticipation of when she'd be able to chew her nails once more. Instead, she was working carefully to keep something alive.

The Makeshift Carrier

It wasn't until after Michael moved upstairs that he and Eric realized that the attic bedroom was not connected to the house's main duct work. As a show of good faith, and to keep ice from forming on the inside of the window, Eric purchased an oil-filled radiator off Craigslist. It only cost $20, but the on/off switch was broken, which meant Michael could use it running full blast or not at all. This made winter a balancing act for Michael—the radiator inhabiting the far corner of the room near the door and the tiny window next to Michael's bed cracked open whenever the radiator was running.

More often than not, if Michael was reading or doing homework, he kept the window closed and the radiator off, relying instead on the heat from the main part of the house to rise and warm the floor where he sat.

Less a knock on the door and more a brushing of knuckles against the pressboard roused Michael from his favorite section of *A Christmas Carol*, where young Ebenezer Scrooge is reunited with his sister, Fan.

"Come in."

When Claire opened the door, heat and the moist smell of cooking tomato sauce rushed into the room.

"Are you busy?" she asked.

"I should be." Scattered around Michael was a tumble of Dickens novels in various stages of decay—covers creased, pages highlighted and dog-eared. Most sported the bright yellow USED stickers from the university bookstore, with the stickers on *David Copperfield*'s spine three layers thick. "My final is next Wednesday."

"I can come back."

"No. It's all right." Both of Michael's knees creaked when he rose to his feet. "I've spent the last hour rereading *A Christmas Carol*, and that's not even going to be on the final."

Claire's hands withdrew up her sleeves. "It's cold in here."

"It's not so bad closer to the floor."

"Do you have any wool socks?"

Michael shook his head. "So what's up?"

"We got a flyer in the mail from Super Pet Mart. You can get a free picture with Santa with any seven-pound bag of Healthy Kitty Krunch. We needed to get food for Monkey anyways, and I thought I could surprise my brother with the photo."

Eric's cat Monkey was so named because her howling sounded like a viral video of screaming chimpanzees that had been circling the Internet around the time Eric found her roaming homeless in the neighborhood. Monkey was all white with blue eyes and completely deaf. Eric's Googling found that cats with this coloring were three to five times more likely to be deaf than other cats.

It was Monkey's penchant for screaming that inspired Michael to keep the door to his frigid bedroom closed, and even though Google didn't concur, Michael believed her howling sounded so awful because she couldn't hear it herself.

"You need a ride?" Michael asked.

Claire nodded. "If you don't mind and have the time."

Michael glanced out the window—snow was swirling and thick, frosting the cars in the street like uneven layer cakes. His Cavalier parked out front looked like a snowdrift.

"You round up the Monk and I'll start scraping."

§

Eric and Michael had only been living in the house for a few months that summer when Eric came home from work with a six-pack of Grolsch. They'd always been a Budweiser can house, and Michael knew by the condensation fogging the green glass bottles that something momentous was coming. When he took a drink of his beer, he relished the flavor—more complex, with a slight bite that wasn't present in cheap American beer. The bottle's top clinked against the side in a satisfying way.

Instead of taking classes during the summer semester, Michael was doing roofing for his uncle. The work was grueling but satisfying, tearing the degraded shingles off the house, laying new tarpaper, and layering on the new shingles. In the evening, after a shower, Michael baked himself a cook-and-serve lasagna, or he and Eric split a bucket of Church's Chicken. They watched television until bed—reruns of *X-Files* or Eric's DVDs of *Monty Python*—the pain in Michael's upper back and shoulders dulling steadily to a mild ache, so he could climb the ladder to the roofs the next day.

Eric was still wearing the bright blue polo shirt and khakis of his Best Buy uniform. From his place on the couch, Michael imagined he could smell the air conditioning and ozone of new electronics coming off Eric, just as potent as the sunshine and sweat baked into his own clothing.

"I talked to my mom today," Eric said, taking a drink from his beer. "Claire-Bear's boyfriend got her pregnant."

Michael knew what this meant for Eric's sister Claire. It was a common story—she and her boyfriend would buy a small house in Taylor or Trenton with dirty aluminum siding, they would work several part-time jobs to make ends meet, they would scrimp and save to send their children to the same Catholic school they'd gone to, the same school where Michael and Eric met, played hooky, and graduated. Like many of the girls in Eric and Michael's graduating class, Claire would never leave Downriver.

"What'd your mom say?" Michael asked.

"She and Claire've been fighting nonstop. I mean, Claire wasn't planning to go to college or anything, but at least before she had options."

Michael hadn't seen Claire in years—not since he and Eric had moved out to Grand Rapids, Michael for school and Eric for a change of scenery. After a year, Eric liked it so much that he sunk his savings into a house, and now Michael was renting from him and paying half the utilities. Michael remembered Claire as scrawny—all bruised legs and bony wrists, a crooked front tooth.

When he and Eric were in middle school, before drivers' licenses could open up their world to include coffee shops and the mall, the two of them explored on Huffy mountain bikes with sturdy steel frames. They never went far—to the park attached to the elementary school, to Rick's, a corner liquor store where they spent their allowances on candy, pop, and little cardboard boxes of Super Loud Bang Snaps.

One time, a nine-year-old Claire wanted to join them, and when Eric told her "No way!" she cried to their mother.

"Just let your sister ride bikes with you. It won't kill you," his mother had said, exasperated. Tired.

As Claire pedaled furiously to keep up with them, Michael watched how her thin blond hair fanned out from her head, not like the white and purple streamers in her bike's handle bars, but like threads of delicate silk, her scalp showing pink in places. He tried to imagine her pregnant, but the image wouldn't form—she had the skin, bones, and nakedness of a baby bird, too delicate to support another life.

"Anyway," Eric continued, "that's what I wanted to talk to you about. Claire-Bear's boyfriend still lives with his folks, and his Taco Bell job won't be able to support them any time soon. Mom asked if Claire could stay with us for a while."

"Of course. I mean, it's your house."

"Yeah, I know." Eric put his beer on the coffee table, an alley find with scarred legs, brass hardware, and milky rings from sweating beers. He rose to his feet and paced, but Michael knew it wasn't in an effort to find the words, but to find the courage to say them— knowing Eric, he had probably spent all afternoon deciding what he was going to say. "I know I technically own the house, but we both live here. I don't want you to agree because you have to. I'd like you to be okay with it."

Michael resisted the urge to smile. Earnest pleas were one of the things he appreciated about Eric. Eric's tone and furrowed brow had been exactly the same in ninth grade, when Eric asked Michael if he could take Sandy Jenkins to homecoming, the girl Michael had had a crush on in middle school.

"Dude, I'm okay with it."

"To be honest, I don't think things are going to be that different with her here. And once the baby comes… Well, my mom says Claire won't want to be away from home once the baby comes."

"Man, that's weird. I mean, it's one thing to think about your sister being pregnant. It's a whole other story when you think there'll be a baby where no baby existed before."

"Tell me about it. Mom says Claire's boyfriend is an only child, so they'll probably ask me to be the godfather when the baby gets baptized. How's that for a trip?" When Eric resumed drinking, his forehead was still crinkled with worry, but Michael thought he saw a far-away smile in-between sips.

It was decided that Claire would take the Mega Bus from Downtown into Grand Rapids in two weeks. It was enough time for her to get her things in order and for Eric and Michael to prepare for her arrival, which included Michael moving his things from the smaller ground-floor bedroom into the attic room and dragging the futon up from the basement to serve as Claire's bed.

The move upstairs had been Michael's idea, and when Eric protested, he insisted.

"Pretty soon she's going to be carting a lot more of herself around," Michael reasoned as he and Eric negotiated an old queen mattress up the stairs. "She shouldn't have to clomp up and down stairs when she's all pregnant."

"But it's hot up here." The differences in their jobs were apparent—Eric's face was bright red, his breathing heavy, while Michael had hardly broken a sweat. A mattress was nothing compared to a seventy-pound bundle of shingles.

Michael shrugged. "I'll be fine with a fan. And all the more reason not to put a pregnant lady up here."

"Pregnant little girl."

"Pregnant anything. If Monkey was with child, I wouldn't want her padding up and down stairs."

"If Monkey was pregnant, she'd have to, now. How else would she have her litter in the middle of your bed?"

"Funny."

"I've got a million of them."

§

When Claire arrived, she didn't look pregnant. And after a month of living in the house, she still didn't look different. But it wasn't until the three of them sat in the living room for dinner, spaghetti with meatballs Claire had spent all afternoon preparing, that Eric finally said something.

"You think you should go to the doctor? You haven't gained any weight and that can't be healthy. I can take the day off and drive you home if you want."

Michael had had some of the same misgivings, but found himself unable to ask. His image of Eric's little sister was not who had moved into the house—Claire was a stranger. An eighteen-year-old woman had grown out of the baby bird, and she was filled with quiet secrets. In the bathroom, Michael didn't touch her bottles of strawberry shampoo and conditioner, her purple toothbrush. When she left her clothes in the dryer, tank tops and tiny scraps of cotton underwear, Michael did laundry on another day. Once the semester started, Michael was able to spend all of his time at school or in his room, avoiding her almost completely.

He watched then as Claire sighed. She placed her plate on the coffee table, wiped her mouth with a paper napkin, and folded her hands in her lap.

"I'm not pregnant."

"You made it up?"

"No. I was pregnant but I'm not anymore."

"You mean, you got an abortion?" Michael saw Eric's incredulity turn to disgust—eyes narrowed, lips pulled back. Claire's face remained calm.

"Technically, yes. But it wasn't that dramatic. It was just two pills."

"Just two pills? You were having a baby and now you're not, but it was just two pills?"

"And this is why I didn't tell you. I knew you'd wig out." Claire's face was still impassive, but her chest bloomed ruddy and the color started to crawl up her neck.

"I think my little sister, who lives in my house, having an abortion is reason enough for wigging out. Does Mom know? What are you even doing here, then?"

"Dan and I broke up. I was fighting with Mom all the time—I needed a place to stay to figure things out."

"Sounds to me like you already figured things out." When Eric put his plate onto the coffee table, his saucy fork clattered to the floor. An untouched meatball rolled across the table and made a splat when it hit the blue carpeting. Eric stormed out of sight into the kitchen, but Michael heard him grab his keys from the counter and go out the door. Moments later, his car went barreling down the driveway, and Eric was gone.

Claire, meanwhile, had resumed eating her spaghetti, but she had lost her composure—her entire face was red, eyes wide and teary. Besides her sniffling, she and Michael ate in silence.

When Michael's plate was almost empty, Claire asked, "Can I get you more?"

"Naw, I'm good."

"But Eric's spaghetti already has cheese on it." Claire's voice cracked and suddenly the tears were more than she could blink back, huge tears that left snail trails down her cheeks, falling one after another onto her plate when she didn't wipe them away.

"I'll eat it." Michael picked up Eric's cold plate of spaghetti and began shoveling nests of noodles into his mouth. "See? It's fine."

Michael didn't know why Claire was so disturbed by Eric's leftover pasta, but to Michael's relief, she stopped crying and seemed to calm down as he ate it.

§

Despite the weather, Super Pet Mart was swarmed with people. Michael and Claire stood at the end of a very long line crammed with pet owners holding cat carriers or with their dogs on leashes, sweating in their winter coats. Michael saw one dog licking at a salty, dirt puddle forming around its owner's shoes and had to look away.

"Couldn't you find Monkey's carrier?" Michael asked.

"I looked and looked and didn't find one," Claire said. She held a blue plastic laundry basket to her chest covered with a towel held in place by a bungee cord. Monkey's face was pressed against the side, her pink nose poking out and quivering. "Besides, I thought this was a pretty clever makeshift cat carrier."

"You want me to hold it?"

"Not yet. We're probably going to have to be here awhile, and I might ask you to hold it later. Besides, you'll have to carry the food." Claire poked her head out of line to count the people ahead of them. "I had no idea it was going to be this crazy."

"I guess everyone had the same thought you did."

"But what's Eric going to do with all those pictures of strangers' pets?"

"Funny."

"I've got a million of them." She looked at the line in front of them once more, as if to be sure that there really were that many people ahead of them. "If we're real late, I won't have dinner ready before Eric gets home."

"What're you cooking tonight?"

The moment Claire arrived, she took over the kitchen, making use of the pots and pans that previously had been purely decorative. Eric and Michael hadn't ordered pizza, or picked up Church's Chicken, or eaten take-out burritos in months. Claire threw out the frozen meals and cans of Spaghetti-Os, replacing them with bulbs of garlic, bottles of olive oil, jars of olives. She made pasta puttanesca. She made beef stroganoff. Once she roasted a whole chicken, served it with mashed potatoes and pan gravy, and made soup the next day from the carcass.

The Santa line inched forward.

"Well, I made a fresh pot of sauce today, so we could have pasta," Claire said. "But I also have some capers and thought it might be nice to try making chicken piccatta."

"I don't even know what capers are," Michael said.

"Sure you do. Little green berry-type things? Taste briney?" Michael shook his head.

"Well, they're delicious," Claire assured him.

"If we get back too late for the chicken, I'm sure the pasta will be good. Or we could order in. You don't have to cook all the time, you know."

"I like it. I like feeling like I'm taking care of you guys. Especially when I'm not working yet. I might as well play 'happy homemaker.' I can get some high heels and pearls and vacuum Donna Reed-style."

"How do you even know who Donna Reed is?"

"Internet memes."

Michael knew it bothered Eric that Claire remained jobless. Eric was biting his tongue in the hopes Claire would decide to go to school. That didn't keep him from snapping at both Claire and Michael when he got annoyed. With the holidays approaching, he'd been home even less, picking up extra shifts to stay out of the house.

"Can't you play up college to her?" Eric asked while he and Michael did the dishes one night. Michael was washing while Eric dried and put away. During dinner, Claire had been inspired to bake an apple pie, and she was out at the store to pick up the ingredients. "Tell her it's a great time."

"'A great time?' I think college is one of those things you have to want to do."

"Well, at least if she goes to college, one good thing will come out of this whole abortion fiasco." Eric dried the last fork, dropped it into the tray, and slammed the drawer closed.

Michael pulled the sink drain and wrung out the sponge, placed the sponge on the special antibacterial holder Claire'd purchased. "I don't get it. It wasn't good when Claire got pregnant. But now that she's not pregnant, it's still not good?"

Eric, his lips pursed, went to the refrigerator, took out a Coke and cracked it open. Michael wondered if maybe he was too angry to say anything, but Eric finally said, "It's just why she did it, you know? She breaks up with her boyfriend and decides she's got to get an abortion. Know what it did to my mom? She's told she's going to be a grandmother and then she's just not anymore?"

Michael nodded.

"But you know what pisses me off the most? Claire couldn't trust us. We're her family, we would have been there to help her. Me, Mom—Christ, even you. All these people, but she thinks an abortion is her only option."

Michael spent the evening in his room reading *Oliver Twist*, but he heard Claire return from the store and begin baking the apple pie. He had no idea how late she was up working on it. In the morning, the whole house smelled like baked apples and cinnamon, the buttery-comfort of pie crust—and the realization of how he'd been avoiding Eric's sister since she moved in coated his tongue, the guilt thick and heavy in his stomach.

§

The line moved forward again. From where they stood, Michael could just make out the towers of seven-pound bags of dog and cat food flanking the photography station.

"Hey. Have you ever thought of doing culinary school?"

Claire turned to face him, her eyes narrowed. "Did my brother put you up to this?"

"No. He's hoping you'll choose college. And if you're interested in college, I think you should do it. But if you're not, you seem to like cooking. That might be a good match for you."

"Huh. Maybe. I do love it."

"Did you learn it from your mom?"

"No. I learned it because of my mom—her idea of cooking is to mix together a can of Campbell's soup and noodles and bake it in the oven." When she wrinkled her nose, her pale winter freckles disappeared in the grooves.

"Hey! No knocking tuna noodle casserole. That's the only home cooking we had before you showed up, with your capers and your pasta."

Claire hitched Monkey's basket closer to her chest and fell silent.

Michael went back to noticing how the Christmas carols playing over the sound system sounded tinny and the fluorescent lights made the overcast day outside look darker. As they inched forward, Michael could see Santa, sweat shining around his beard. The store was steamy with wet dog and snow-melted hats. Michael took off his wool coat and pushed up the sleeves of his flannel shirt, but didn't feel any more comfortable.

"I know that Eric thinks I got an abortion because Dan and I broke up."

Michael's attention snapped back to Claire. Her head was down, as if she was seriously considering the balding towel thrown over Monkey's basket. When she looked up, her eyes were twinkling and fierce. "But he's wrong."

"Um." Michael didn't know what to say. He didn't want to have this conversation, but walking away and leaving her didn't seem like an option. He wished he was home, alone, in his chilly bedroom. He looked up at the drop ceiling, stained brown in places where the roof had leaked.

"Dan wanted to keep the baby. I didn't. And I'm not home because my mom wanted me to give it up for adoption."

The redness had started to crawl up Claire's neck, but Michael didn't know if it was from the hot store or because she was upset.

Michael felt like it was his turn to speak, and worried about what would happen if he didn't. "Why didn't you?"

The line moved forward.

"I just couldn't. I couldn't give away my baby. Just leave it? But I'm not ready to be a mom. Not yet. So I went to the clinic, even when I knew the outcome—Mom not forgiving me and Dan not wanting to stay together."

"Did you tell your brother all of this?"

"I shouldn't have to."

For Michael, it was like fitting the last piece of a puzzle into place, or a camera lens auto focusing, or reading the final chapter of a mystery novel, when it becomes clear how all the clues fit together. Both Eric and Claire were operating within the confines of their own understood reality, and neither was willing to let the other in, and he could see it because he was outside of both. He wanted to tell her, but didn't know how, and before he could summon the words, they were at the front of the line, and the moment had passed.

"And who do we have here?" Santa's elf was a Super Pet Mart employee named Sandy, a striped white and green Santa hat with attached elf ears perched on her head and candy canes lining the pocket of her apron.

"This is Monkey," Claire said, removing the bungee cord and towel from the basket and lifting Monkey out. "She's still got her claws, so you'd better let me handle her."

Claire cradled the usually-cantankerous Monkey, who seemed content to sit quietly in her arms, despite the strange surroundings and all the dogs around.

"She's a beautiful cat," Sandy said, and steered Claire into position on Santa's left. "And you can stand here," Sandy said, motioning Michael to Santa's right.

"Oh, no. I'm just the ride."

"Come be in the picture," Claire protested.

He didn't want to be in the picture, but he was aware of the line teeming behind him, and didn't think arguing about it was the best idea. So Michael shrugged, dropped his jacket into Monkey's carrier, and took his place on Santa's right side.

The Super Pet Mart elf snapped the photo without warning. While Claire recaged Monkey, Michael grabbed one of the bags of cat food and made his way to the cash register at the front of the store, hoping that he hadn't ruined the photo by blinking or wearing a stupid face.

"I put Monkey in the basket and bungeed the towel in place

before I realized that your coat is in there," Claire said when she caught up with him in the checkout line. "Wanna help me get it out?"

Michael peered into the side of the laundry basket—Monkey was curled peaceably in the folds of his jacket, and he could already see a fine coating of white hairs against the black wool. She was purring.

"Nah, let her keep it. It's so hot in here I'm looking forward to being cold."

"Hey, I love this song."

Michael listened and could just hear children and John Lennon singing that the war was over if he wanted it before crossing through the super-heated vestibule out into the unusually-dark winter afternoon.

By the time Michael and Claire returned home, Eric was already there, the door of his bedroom closed. Counting Crows could be heard, muffled but distinctly, even in the kitchen.

Claire abandoned her capers, but scratched her cooking itch by slathering sliced baguette with a homemade garlic herb butter and using the broiler to melt parmesan overtop. She piled the garlic bread on a platter that Michael had never seen before and set it in the middle of the kitchen table, which she had cleared of the pieces of junk mail, papers, and other various bits of their lives that usually didn't have a place to go.

Michael watched as she spooned the spaghetti with her tomato sauce into elaborate nests on three plates, folded paper towels into triangles, and put a fork and spoon at each place setting. She then took a seat, motioned for Michael to sit, and cast a stricken look toward Eric's door—forehead creased as she chewed her bottom lip. He had obviously heard them return home as clearly as Michael and Claire could hear Adam Duritz singing, but he hadn't emerged to say hello.

Michael only deliberated a moment before striding over to Eric's room and knocking loudly.

"Yeah?" Eric asked when he opened the door.

"It's time to eat, man," Michael said.

Eric's eyes narrowed, and Michael wondered if he was going to be difficult. Instead, Eric walked back into his bedroom, hit the power button on his ancient stereo, and followed Michael into the kitchen for dinner.

As they ate, Claire didn't say anything about the trip to Super Pet Mart, so Michael didn't, either.

§

On Christmas morning, Claire woke before dawn to make cranberry white chocolate scones and mulled cider. She lit the multi-colored Christmas lights that she'd hung in the living room right after Thanksgiving, and woke Michael and Eric from sleep by blasting the Mormon Tabernacle Choir's version of "Joy to the World."

"You're nuts. You know that, right?" Eric said, but accepted a scone from her just the same.

Michael watched as the pat of butter he'd put on the still-warm scone melted into its crumbly depths. He ate it slowly—the richness of the white chocolate, the tartness from the cranberries, and the salted creaminess of the butter mingled on his tongue in a way that tasted, to Michael, the way all Christmas mornings should taste.

"It's hard to sleep when there are presents to open," Claire said, her mug of cider warming the underside of her nose.

Claire's present to Eric was wrapped in bright gold paper that Monkey stalked after Eric tore it from the box. Inside was a wooden frame with the words *My Family* painted across the top. In the picture, Claire was smiling brightly, Monkey cuddled close to her face, with Michael standing austerely on Santa's other side.

Michael thought about how, before long, he would have to take a shower and drive the two and a half hours to Taylor, to have Christmas dinner with Mom, Dad, and Grandma. His family would ask him about living with Eric and Claire. They would have heard about the abortion—at church, in the line at Kroger—because it was the kind of family secret that leaches into the water of a Downriver community. Michael imagined their righteous indignation eclipsing even curiosity about school and what he planned to do with an English degree.

Michael wished that he could stay—Claire couldn't go home, and Eric was staying with her. She was so excited about the pasta maker that Eric and Michael got for her for Christmas that she was going to make homemade ravioli for dinner, stuffed with pumpkin and cooked with sausage and sage.

"Are your hands clean?" Claire asked.

Michael set his plate down, bare even of crumbs, wiped his hands on his pajama pants, and took the lumpy package from Claire.

The present was a pair of socks that she'd knitted herself—not out of wool, but out of a soft gray acrylic yarn, which Michael wore until the yarn, fuzzed with age, started to pull and run. After that, he kept them balled up in the bottom of his sock drawer.

Sisters

After the biting cold of February, where fingers stung instead of going numb and windshield frost refused to melt, my sister's hospital room was hot and moist. Mary, the morning shift nurse, was checking Sarah's saline bags and morphine drip. Sarah's snoring was rhythmic and deep—two sharp intakes followed by an exhausted exhalation—perfectly in step with the humming humidifier and beeping monitors. The music of hospice.

"Good morning, Miss Shoal," Mary said when I entered. "We haven't woken up since yesterday."

Mary was a strong woman in her thirties; stout, we would have called her in my day. I was sure the nurses were trained in that way, but I still appreciated her use of "we."

"We haven't eaten anything today."

"Our urine was dark yesterday."

"We're not in any pain."

Even when I couldn't be at Sarah's side, I knew she wasn't alone.

Mary lifted Sarah's body easily with one arm, so she could rearrange her pillows and straighten her gown.

After Mary left, I removed my coat and sweater, placed my knitting on the chair near Sarah's bed, and opened the shade. Thin sunlight filtered through the condensation beaded on the window and gilded the simple crucifix hung over Sarah's bed. A white film crusted the corners of my sister's open mouth, coating her tongue. I wet one of the small sponges on a stick with water from the yellow plastic carafe and cleared the crust away.

Before the morphine, before "It won't be long now," I was more useful. I could talk with my sister, hold her hand. She knew I was there to comfort her. Now she was unaware of everything—the tubes, the antiseptic smell, the blankets and sheets heavy with damp.

Crushed against her head, Sarah's hair looked mousy and thin. Before she got sick, Sarah kept a hair appointment every six weeks for years, to dye it auburn, to tease it out into a style Jackie Kennedy would have admired. The morphine made Sarah's face slack. The hairs on her upper lip had turned coarse and dark.

I felt the need to care about these things for her—the disintegration of her body, the mortifications of her illness. She was always so careful with her skin and clothes, but I didn't know where to start, or how to take over these ministrations.

§

During the summer of 1945, after the *Detroit Free Press* announced that Hitler was dead, but before the U.S. dropped the atomic bomb on Hiroshima, I told my parents and Sarah of my plans to join the Felician Sisters.

We were sitting in the first-floor dining room at the Detroit Yacht Club after spending the morning on the beach. A particularly sharp grain of sand had made its way into my shoe and torn my nylon stockings, garnering censure from my mother.

"Who wears stockings to the beach?" she said, shaking her head. She poured my sister and me cups of tea from the silver pot before serving herself. My father was sipping a Manhattan, holding the maraschino cherry in place with his finger so it wouldn't bob against his lip. Before his cocktail was finished, Sarah would reach across the table, pluck the cherry from his drink and eat it, which always made my father laugh, no matter how many times she did it.

"Had you brought your swimsuit, you would've been in the water and saved your stockings," Sarah said, her arm thrown languidly over the back of her chair, her gaze trained on the docks.

"I have an extra pair of cotton ones you can wear to dinner this evening," Mother said and stirred milk into her tea.

"Nonsense," Sarah said. Talk of cotton stockings was enough to pull her attention from the young men working on boats docked at the pier. "It's summer, and those cotton stockings are horrible. She can wear mine—I'll go without."

"Sarah!" Mother admonished.

"It's the fashion."

Sarah often used this reasoning to get her way. "It was the fashion" to wear the two-piece bathing suits my mother felt were too immodest for a girl of fifteen, "it was the fashion" to smell of singed hair and my father's pomade, to wear lipstick, despite the fear that people would consider her, in my mother's words, "a loose and immoral girl."

I had let her put some of it on me, and in the teapot's surface, my mouth stretched huge and red in my distorted face.

Drinking tea in the middle of the afternoon felt decadent after my work with the Sisters. I'd started volunteering after school and on the weekends when I turned sixteen—doing laundry, washing the floors and windows in their quarters. After I graduated, I was brought on in a more permanent role, with duties that included preparing and serving meals. When not on holiday, the three o'clock hour would be spent peeling potatoes, kneading bread dough, or running to the market for the head cook.

I had only been away for a few days, but I desperately missed them—their quiet and companionship. The order to their lives. The Felician Sisters in the central convent prayed, ate, and, in the Holy Mother's words, "recreated together," and I already felt a part of it.

These last few days on Belle Isle had been a strange combination of harried aimlessness, during which my parents catered constantly to Sarah's whims—beach days, lunches at the club, attending evening dances like the one tonight.

Sarah turned a fierce eye on me. After the beach, she'd spent the better part of an hour fixing her hair. Instead of looking comical, the lipstick on her face only highlighted her youthful prettiness. She thought herself sultry, like Hedy Lamar—but she always made me think of Vivien Leigh, with her disdainful nose and pouty ways that were the torment of the boys vacationing with their parents.

"Speaking of, which dress will you be wearing with my stockings?" she asked.

"The black taffeta, probably."

"Just because you work with a bunch of nuns doesn't mean you have to dress like one."

"Sarah! A little respect. Your sister's work is admirable," Mother said.

"And not done," I said. "I spoke to the Holy Mother before we left. I told her that I thought it was time to deepen my involvement with their order." My stomach squirmed. "She agreed, and said that the years I have spent in their service were a type of 'candidacy.' With your and father's blessing, I have been invited to enter into the postulancy."

"Oh, Arlene," my mother's voice cracked. She grasped my hand tightly. "We are so happy for you."

"No!" Sarah pushed hastily from the table, upsetting her teacup and smacking her chair into the wall. "You're not going to let her do this, are you?" she demanded of my father, her face flushed and her hands curled into tiny fists.

"Sit down," my father said quietly. "Arlene has been called by God, and we will be happy for her."

"I won't. 'Calling' my foot!" Sarah turned to me, eyes red-rimmed and angry. "You're just scared. Of living. Of everything. With your dowdy dresses, your books on the beach. You'll regret this, Arlie."

After her speech, Sarah ran from the room. I wanted to follow and make her understand that I wasn't giving something up—but I knew I couldn't. Sarah had never felt out of place in her life. Every look, every move that she made, was always exactly how it was supposed to be. I knew she would find love, would get married and start a family, and these things would make her happy. How could I make her understand that a life with the Sisters was the only one that made sense to me?

The diners were few, but those present were staring. I saw my mother reign in her horror and give a little laugh.

"Young girls are so excitable these days," she said liltingly to an older couple dining at the nearest table. The woman nodded her gray head in sympathy.

"Don't let Sarah's outburst ruin this for you, Arlie," my father said, draining his drink. "She's young and can't understand your devotion to something outside yourself."

"And she's losing a sister, dear," my mother said. She patted my arm with a trembling hand. I looked at the smear of red on the rim of my teacup and felt sick.

§

A few days after the funeral, *The Price is Right* was playing on the television in the other room, and I was preparing lunch–a ham and cheese sandwich on white bread, canned tomato soup–when the movers arrived.

I opened the door to a burly man standing next to a handcart stacked with boxes.

"You Arlene Shoal?" he asked, consulting his clipboard. "Where do you want them?"

"Stacked in the sitting room here, please."

He left the handcart on the stoop and carried the boxes inside—perhaps the wheels of the handcart were wet from the snow, or the cart would have been difficult to maneuver over my beige carpeting. The man was careful to wipe his feet on the welcome mat before stepping in.

He made seven trips in all—stacking the boxes two deep in front of my credenza.

"Sign here," he said, indicating a line at the bottom of a pale yellow form. He had broken a sweat while carrying the boxes and I could smell the heat of him, wrapped inside a fleece-lined jacket, stronger than my simmering soup. I wrote my name slowly, perfectly forming the intricate cursive "S" in Shoal. I didn't often get to sign for things.

After he was gone, I surveyed the room—my couch and end table with lamp, the over-stuffed blue recliner that had been a gift from Sarah and Rick on my sixtieth birthday, the television, its stand completely hidden behind boxes. The room had never looked so full.

§

In 1975, after almost thirty years, I left the Felician Sisters.

Our community had been operating in a school just outside of New Jersey, working as teachers and spiritual leaders. My subject was history. But the school was experiencing decreased enrollment, and the state decided to consolidate and close our school.

"We are still needed as a pillar in this community," our Holy Mother explained when she made the announcement. "We will continue our work at a clinic near Columbus Park. Those with medical training will serve as nurses, the rest will counsel patients and their families."

With the announcement, I felt a weight in my chest that I couldn't reconcile. I prayed for guidance, but was afraid of the answers I found there.

Finally, I sought an audience with the Holy Mother. She looked incongruous sitting at her institutional desk—a soft-lined face in the traditional habit and veil against green-painted metal and dark Formica. Early morning sun slanted through the high window, sparkling the few dust motes dancing in the air.

"Sister Arlene, what's troubling you?"

"I'm afraid I have made a mistake." Despite my resolve, there was a catch in my throat. I blinked furiously to keep away tears. "I love teaching, and since the news of our new calling, a disappointment has settled in my heart that I have been unable to shake."

"A love of teaching is noble," the Holy Mother said. "Perhaps, in time, you will also learn to love nursing."

"That's just it. Prior to this, I feel as if I'd gone untested. My love of teaching and my faith had always traveled the same path, and I never had to think about which was stronger. After many hours of meditation and prayer, I fear my desire to teach outweighs my desire to serve God in whatever capacity he calls me to."

The Holy Mother folded her hands, knuckles swollen with arthritis, veins starkly blue beneath her skin. "The time you have spent in community with us should not be seen as a mistake," she said finally. "You have devoted yourself to the teachings of God and the education of his children. Should you find that now you must travel a different path, your Sisters will miss you, but we will know that you go in faith."

When I called Sarah and told her I was leaving the convent, she didn't ask me to explain. She didn't try to talk me out of my decision and she didn't sympathize. Instead, she and Rick bought me a plane ticket, picked me up from the airport, and drove me in the Mustang to their house in Southfield.

It was only the second time I'd been in their house since she and Rick had built it. The echoey vestibule with the high ceiling, the large white-carpeted stairs leading up to the second floor, and the marble tiled floors were just as impressive the second time around.

"Are you hungry?" Sarah asked. From the kitchen, I could hear Rick pad up the stairs with my two suitcases. "We'll eat dinner in a few hours, but if you're hungry now, I can fix you a sandwich or a TV dinner."

I thought about the Sisters—the three o'clock hour on a Saturday would be used for personal prayer.

"I can wait," I said and took a seat on one of the bar stools. Sarah's kitchen was bright and modern, with little yellow flowers on the wallpaper and bright white Formica countertops. The stool I sat on had slender teak legs and was upholstered in rough yellow fabric.

"Hi, Aunt Arlie."

Barbara, Sarah and Rick's only child, stood in the kitchen doorway. She was tall and angular like her father, but had Sarah's features, a softness at the jaw and large, staring eyes. I got up from my seat and hugged her. I only came up to her chin.

"You're a great grown girl of fifteen now?" I asked. She was only ten years old when I saw her last. Besides her height, she'd let her hair grow long. It was thick and dark like Rick's had been when he was younger and courting Sarah.

"Almost sixteen," she said with pride. She walked to the refrigerator and pulled out a bottle of Coca Cola. "Would you like one?"

The last time I'd had a Coke was three years before, while suffering from indigestion. A few bottles were always kept on hand to help with mild stomach upsets.

Reminding myself that I wasn't beholden to the same rules as before, I said, "If I could, just a splash of yours, dear," and tried not to feel guilty.

Barbara took a juice glass from the cupboard and measured exactly half of her Coke into it. "How long you staying?" she asked, handing me the glass.

"A few weeks," Sarah chimed in. She'd been wiping down the spotless counter with a dishcloth. "Dad's looking for a condo for her, and she'll stay with us until he finds one."

§

Sarah went into the hospital after she broke her hip. She pulled the phone down off the hall table across from the staircase. I pictured her splayed across the marble floor, cold through the fine fabrics of her clothing.

"My sandal got caught in the carpet and I fell all the way down. I think I broke my leg, maybe my hip," she said matter-of-factly, but her breath had the shallow hiss of pain.

"I'll be there in fifteen minutes," I said, slipping into my shoes and grabbing the car keys from the hook by the door.

"Meet me at Providence. I called 911 first."

"I can be there quicker."

"And what will you do when you get here?" she snapped. "You won't know how to move me and I can't move myself. Just meet me in the ER."

I didn't want to hang up the phone until the ambulance got there. "Do you want me to call Barbara?" Barbara was now Dr. Aiken, practicing internal medicine in Sierra Leone, Africa, with the Doctors Without Borders program.

"And worry her?" The edge was gone from Sarah's voice, leaving it tired and scared. "Let's wait and see what we're up against first."

We learned we were up against Dedifferentiated Chondrosarcoma—tumors in Sarah's bones, first discovered while doctors were x-raying her hip to assess the damage.

The oncologist was young, with a serious face and quiet hands. He kept his fingers interlaced but absently touched his plain gold wedding band from time to time.

"Our treatment options are limited, due to the way the cancer has metastasized," he said quietly. "Amputation is not an option at this point, and chemotherapy has never proven effective at treating this disease. We may consider radiation."

I was holding Sarah's hand on top of the white hospital blanket. Her fingers were cool and gripped mine lightly.

"Thank you, Dr. Brown," Sarah said, as if we were all attending one of her polite parties, and Dr. Brown had just informed her that the cheese ball needed more crackers. "My daughter is a doctor. She'll be here in the morning, and I think it would be best to discuss treatment options then."

"Of course," Dr. Brown said. He rose to his feet, shook Sarah's hand and then my own. His palms were sweaty.

Sarah and I sat in silence for a while. She had her face toward the window which framed the tops of the maple trees shading the parking lot. In the thinning October sun, the topmost leaves had started to yellow, standing out starkly against a blue blue sky without clouds.

Sarah's room was not unlike the one I'd had with the Felician Sisters—bare walls, a bed, a nightstand, a chair. With the television off, it was easy to forget it was there. The familiarity was comforting.

"It doesn't seem real," Sarah said finally, still turned toward the window.

I nodded, even though she wasn't looking.

"It was nothing. Pins and needles if I sat too long. A little bit of swelling and soreness. I took an Aleve and thought it was nothing. I thought, 'I'm old. I'm finally getting arthritis. It won't kill me.'"

I gave Sarah's hand a squeeze. She didn't hold mine back, but she did turn to look at me.

"I'm never going to leave this bed," she said.

"Wait until Barbara comes, then discuss the treatment options," I said, trying to sound earnest and upbeat, not wanting to betray the dread that had settled like a ball of cold phlegm in my stomach. "You can't know what's going to happen."

"Can't I?"

§

With a reference letter from Bishop Lucas, the head of the Apostolate, I was able to procure a position as a seventh-grade history teacher at Baker Junior High, a public school surrounded by chain link fences and overlooking the expressway. Ninety-five percent of the students were black, and all of them were poor.

The principal instituted monthly drills—for fire and severe weather, but after the Detroit riots only a few years before, there were also drills for gang violence and shootings. When the siren sounded for the gang-riot drills, the students and I slid off our chairs and folded up under our desks. Unlike the chatter that inevitably accompanied the fire drills, the gang-violence siren inspired silence.

To celebrate my "successful reentry" as Rick called it, Sarah threw a small party in my honor.

I wore a green turtleneck sweater with a tartan wool skirt. The only jewelry I owned was a gold crucifix, a gift from my mother for my Perpetual Profession. I put it on, regarded my reflection in the bathroom mirror, decided the crucifix made me look more austere than festive, and took it off again. I wanted Sarah to know that I was at least trying.

The party took place in the basement—Rick presided behind the wet bar, looking dapper in a pale blue suit. Sarah wore a white halter-top, exposing delicate shoulders still bronzed from the summer sun. There were some couples and, I realized quickly, some men present without dates. I didn't know anyone except Sarah and Rick.

"Where's Barbara?" I asked Sarah, who was putting out a tray of deviled eggs, topped with green olive slices.

"She's staying at a friend's house tonight. This is a grown-up party." Sarah fixed a fierce eye on me, and I tried to smile. I had already begun to sweat in my sweater. "Go ask Rick to fix you a drink."

"Here's the guest of honor!" Rick said when I approached. "What'll it be, Arlie?"

"I guess I'm not sure." I hadn't been a drinker before joining the Sisters. After, I even abstained from the sacramental wine during mass, which was sweet like grape juice.

"How about a Tequila Sunrise?" Before I could respond, Rick started to measure juice, alcohol, and syrup into a glass. Even though he was almost completely gray, my sister's husband had a young and kind face, with a tiny black mustache and firm jaw. He presented the drink to me with a paper umbrella and a straw, and smiled when I took a sip.

"Good, huh?" he asked.

It tasted like orange and cherry candies. I nodded.

"You settling in?"

"Oh, the condo is wonderful," I said. "So much space! I don't know what to do with it all."

"Give it time. You'll figure it out."

"I really appreciate how much you, and Sarah, have done for me since I arrived," I said. I could feel my face getting hot, either from my debt to my sister's husband or the tequila.

"We're family, and you do for family," Rick said firmly, then waved to the far end of the room. "Hey, Danny! Come meet my sister-in-law!"

Danny's silk shirt, open at the neck to reveal a heavy gold chain and chest hair, was emblazoned with large brown flowers. The hand clutching his beer wore three gold rings that clinked against the glass.

"So you're the teacher?" he said, his smile full of teeth.

"Arlene," I replied, offering my hand. He pumped it enthusiastically, which sloshed my drink.

"So, you used to be a nun, huh?"

"A Felician Sister."

"That's wild! Why'd you quit?"

I didn't know how to respond. I didn't feel comfortable being there with all those strangers, and certainly wasn't comfortable talking about my life decisions with Danny, his comb over, and his chest hair. I shrugged.

"Rick says you took a job in a Negro school. That ought to be interesting. You guys should do what the nuns used to do in MY day, and hit the kids with switches."

I sipped my drink and didn't respond. After a moment, Danny openly looked me over, glanced over at Sarah, and excused himself.

I don't remember much of the evening after that. There were more Tequila Sunrises, and at one point, Rick danced me around across the basement. I collided with the pool table and bruised my hip.

"Do you like this song?" Rick asked.

I tried to listen, but all I heard was strangers talking, the clicking of high heels on the tile floor.

"It's a Mamas and the Papas album. We'll have to get you a record player."

Long before the party was over, Sarah had to help me up the basement stairs, up the white-carpeted stairs, to the master bathroom, so I could be sick in peace. I am not sure how long I was in there, but I know that later, after there was nothing else to bring up and I was lying with my face on the cool tile floor, Sarah knocked softly on the door and whispered "I'm sorry" when I didn't answer.

§

When I entered the kitchen of the funeral home, Barbara was there, sitting at a table laden with deli trays, relish trays, trays of bagels, all wrapped in plastic and untouched. Her black dress made her tanned skin look sallow and highlighted the circles under her eyes.

"Are you hungry?" Barbara asked, moving to remove the plastic from the nearest tray.

"No, thank you, dear."

"Me neither." Barbara slumped back into her seat and took a sip of coffee. When I took one of the white Styrofoam cups from the stack, Barbara said, "This coffee is terrible. I'm pretty sure it curdled the cream when I poured it in."

"I never drink coffee," I replied and filled the cup with tap water.

"There's bottled water in the refrigerator."

"This is just fine." I took a seat across from her.

"We only drink bottled water in Sierra Leone," she said, staring into her coffee cup. "Nothing else is really safe."

At almost fifty, Barbara was still unmarried. She never lost her angular frame, but the stress of her work in Africa was apparent in other ways—deep lines around the eyes and mouth, a permanently furrowed forehead—signs of aging familiar from my own face. But when she smiled, she still looked so much like Sarah.

"Are you hiding in here?" I asked her finally.

She gave a short laugh, suddenly her father's daughter. "I am trying to convince myself to not feel guilty."

"Is it working?"

Barbara shook her head.

"No one can stop cancer."

"I just keep thinking, had I been here, maybe I would've noticed something. They might've been able to treat it, had it been caught sooner. I've spent so much of my life taking care of strangers halfway around the world, but I couldn't take care of my own mother."

"Your mother was so proud of the work you do. 'My daughter the doctor.' Besides, when God calls us to work, there is really only one answer."

"I guess you know that first hand, huh, Aunt Arlie?"

"Very much so."

We sat quietly for a few minutes more while I finished my water.

"How long will you stay, after the funeral?" I finally asked.

"A week or so. I've already met with the lawyer. When I wasn't at the hospital with Mom, I started going through the house. There's so much stuff."

"Your mother lived in that house for most of her life."

In 1988, while Barbara was completing her residency, a semi-truck merged into Rick's Mustang on the expressway. The ensuing crash involved a dozen cars. Rick died at the scene.

"She wouldn't leave that house after Dad died," Barbara said, shaking her head. "Why didn't she ask you to move in with her?"

"She did. But I'm an old woman and set in my ways."

"It's too big for one person. I tried as recently as last Christmas to get her to sell it, but she wouldn't budge. Stubborn."

"Your father built that house for her."

Barbara sighed, raked her hands through her hair. "I'm going to have to sell it, Aunt Arlie. I feel sick about it, but what am I going to do with a house in Michigan?"

"You have all sorts of guilt visiting you today."

Her smile was small and sad. "I'll be donating most of the furniture and things. Some pieces that I'm inordinately fond of, like the kitchen bar stools and the chest of drawers in my room, I'll put into storage. But here's the thing, Mom had already started to box stuff up, before the accident. Before she knew about the cancer."

I thought back to the day we learned about Dedifferentiated Chondrosarcoma and Sarah's certainty that she'd never go home again.

"There are a few boxes with your name on them," Barbara continued.

"Really?"

"Before things got really bad with Mom, I asked her about them. She said it's stuff she wants you to have. I don't know what all of it is, but I do know that there are some pieces of jewelry that used to be Grandma's."

"You should take these things. What is an old lady going to do with jewelry?"

Barbara smiled. "If you figure it out, let me know. And I'm taking some pieces—both of their wedding rings, the gigantic ruby pendant dad bought Mom for their twenty-fifth wedding anniversary. That stuff I will actually be taking back with me. But in the next couple of days, movers will be coming to haul everything away, and I was going to have them drop your boxes off to you."

I sighed.

"It's completely up to you, but Mom was pretty insistent that your boxes go to you. You could always donate the stuff inside later. Will you take them?"

"I will."

§

It's after dinner and *Wheel of Fortune* is on. The boxes stacked in front of the television are higher than the credenza, and from my seat on the couch, I can't see the contestants' totals. I find that it doesn't make much of a difference.

Despite time being heavy on my hands since Sarah's passing, I'm trying to decide when to call the rectory. Father Burgess of St. Anne's has been such a help. He didn't bat an eye when I told him I would need to take a break from my Eucharistic Minister duties on Sundays and teaching catechism to the fourth graders preparing for their First Holy Communion on Wednesdays, even though I'm sure it was hard to find a replacement at the last minute.

Father Burgess even came to the hospital to perform the anointing of the sick on Sarah. I need to write him a thank you note.

I should call the church and let them know that I will be able to return to my duties. That I'm looking forward to resuming my role as an active member of the community.

Just thinking about it makes me tired.

While I wasn't paying attention to the program, Pat Sajack read the bonus round clue, about a 1983 Pulitzer Prize-winning novel written in the form of letters to the protagonist's sister and to God. The contestant's three consonants and one vowel were hidden behind the boxes.

"I guess it's time for bed, then," I say aloud and turn off the television, but instead of heading to the bathroom, I sit, listening to the fizzle and pop of the television dying.

The only light in the apartment is the soft glow from the brass table lamp. Without the television screen backlighting them, the seven boxes seem huge, as quiet and expecting as Sarah's ghost.

"All right, Sarah," I say to the boxes. "All right."

With the scissors from my sewing basket, I cut the tape on the first box. Lying on top, and smelling strongly of mothballs, is Sarah's mink fur stole. I lift it out and touch it—the fur is still soft, but the lining has stiffened with age. Beneath the stole is a riot of color— gloves, scarves, and hats, fashion spanning decades. Here is the mink fur muff to match the stole, a pair of white velvet gloves that come all the way to the elbow, which Sarah wore exactly once, to a showing of *Suor Angelica*. She wrote to me about the performance in one of her letters.

I slice open a second box, and find this one filled with smaller boxes. One near the top is ornately carved and smells of sandalwood. When I open it, it's velvet lined and contains the jewelry pieces Barbara mentioned—a cameo in an ornate gold frame, the silhouette pictured wearing a diamond studded necklace; a pair of emerald drop earrings; a bracelet made of linked flowers, covered in diamonds— pieces that my mother kept hidden under the mattress, refusing to sell them during The Depression. Any other history these pieces might possess died with her over sixty years ago.

Hidden beneath the jewelry box is a small rectangle, protected carefully by a silk scarf. When I unwrap it, I see it's a picture frame, the silver heavy and in need of polishing. The photo is of Sarah and me, the day of Barbara's baptism. Sarah is wearing a pink checked dress. Her gloved hands are hidden beneath Barbara's christening gown. Standing next to her, I look grim, despite the fact that I am smiling. My white veil and habit look like a hole in the photo where my body should be, and I wonder if this is why Sarah never showed me the picture.

I place the photo on top of the television. Then I affix the cameo brooch to my blouse. I drape the mink stole around my fleshy shoulders and pull the white velvet opera gloves up to my elbows. Thus bedecked, I walk to the bathroom.

Turning on the light, I look at myself in the mirror and wish my sister were here to tell me what I am seeing.

I Don't Belong Here

At the Oakland Square Bed, Bath and Beyond, the candle section is right at the front of the store. With Back to School behind us, looking forward to Halloween, then Thanksgiving into Christmas, the summer scents like Beach Walk and Coastal Waters have been replaced with Pumpkin Pie and Hot Spiced Cider—so that when I open the door at 8 a.m., I am met with a waft of cinnamon. Throughout the course of the day, the festive-cinnamon-smell will work its way into my hair and clothes, making my bedroom hamper smell, at least until the end of the 75% Off Post-Holiday Sale.

Even though it has made getting my boys onto the school bus a hassle, I do like the half hour in the morning before the other team members arrive. I make a clockwise circuit around the store—starting in kitchenware and ending up in bathroom linens, to see which sections were left a mess by the closing crew the night before, which areas need to be restocked or dusted, what signage needs to be swapped out or end caps redesigned. I sip hazelnut coffee from the double-walled stainless steel tumbler I bought when it went on clearance in July. It has a bright orange grip—I liked the lemon-colored one better, but by waiting until the last minute, I was able to get a $20 insulated mug for only $3.99 with my employee discount.

Without the in-store radio playing, which in a few weeks will be all Christmas music all the time, I can hear the heat rattling in the ducts. The sound reverberates in the ceiling, which is high and white-painted, with exposed pipes like the ceiling in the Barry Elementary School gymnasium.

Corporate keeps track of what time the alarm is turned off in the morning, so I leave the house at 7:40, even though work is only ten minutes away, to make sure I am always here on time, even when traffic is backed up for four blocks with folks trying to get on the expressway.

My sons David, seven, and Gary, nine, stay with Mrs. Sawicki next door until the bus comes at 8:05. Mrs. Sawicki's wardrobe is made entirely of pastel-colored nylon robes with front pockets containing safety pins, Kleenex, and crumpled packages of her beloved Doral cigarettes. The robe she was wearing this morning was pink and had scratchy-looking yellow lace around the neck. She held the door open for the boys with one blue-veined hand, a lit cigarette smoldering in the other.

"You know where the TV and cookies are," Mrs. Sawicki said. The boys trooped into her vestibule, shedding their shoes and jackets. "You gotta minute for coffee, Amber?"

She always asks, the dear, even though I never have a minute.

"Not today. Thanks for keeping an eye on them."

"They're good boys," she said, taking a drag from her cigarette and ashing it carefully into the box hedge next to the door. "They're keeping an eye on me."

"Is there anything I can bring you after work?"

In return for Mrs. Sawicki watching the boys in the morning, I give her full reign over my BBB employee discount. I also sometimes run to the drugstore for her during the week—she doesn't drive, and her daughter Marcia only comes on Saturday to take her to the beauty parlor and to the grocery store.

"I saw in the circular that summer entertaining's on clearance.

You still have those matching plastic placemat and chair cushion sets?" Mrs. Sawicki asked.

"I think the turquoise is sold out, but we might still have some in orange or lime."

"If you've got the orange, will you pick me up four? I put them on my kitchen chairs—they're made for outside so they don't stain. Hold on, I'll give you the money."

I shook my head and started for the car. "After my discount on the clearance price, they'll be almost free."

The clearance section is a mess—last night's closing shift didn't even attempt to straighten up before they left. I take a drink of my coffee, which is still steaming hot, and make a mental note to get Kelly on it as soon as she gets in, and to talk to Vince, the store manager, about how the closing shifts are leaving the store.

With some digging, I locate the last four orange placemat cushion sets for Mrs. Sawicki and stick them behind the far register so I can buy them before leaving for the day. They won't be very cheap, but I'm glad to do little things like this for her. Before she started watching the boys, I had to drop them off at school early. Gary and David had to wait for school to start in the gymnasium, with the other children whose parents worked early shifts. They were given granola bars and that horrible-tasting orange juice in the plastic cups with foil tops. All of the kids looked so neglected, and guilt sat stone-like in my stomach every time I dropped them off.

Mrs. Sawicki might smell like cigarettes and Ponds cold cream, but she always has Stella Doro breakfast treats and she lets the boys watch morning cartoons until the bus stops in front of the condominium complex.

At 8:30 on the dot, Kelly walks through the sliding doors. Her bright blue, collared shirt is untucked and both of her eyes look bruised.

"You all right?" I ask.

"You look nice today, too, Amber," Kelly says and then yawns hugely. "What a terrible thing to ask."

"You look like someone punched you in the face twice."

"Oh. It's makeup. It won't come off more than this." She tries rubbing at the skin below her eyes with her shirt, which leaves grey smears on the sleeve but doesn't lessen the bruised look.

I head to the back room to open the safe, Kelly trailing behind me to retrieve her till. "I didn't think you wore makeup."

"I do when I go to City Club. What what!"

"The one in Detroit?"

"Is there another?"

"I can't believe that place is still open. Kids were going there when I was in high school. They used to have a midget in leather doing a trapeze act over the dance floor."

"They still got that on Wednesday nights." Kelly rakes her fingers through her short hair. She normally spikes it, but today it lays soft and flat against her head. "Last night was Heaven or Hell night— I went dressed as a devil with black pleather pants and red sparkle devil horns. Me and Stace were out until three. It was wild."

Stace is Kelly's girlfriend. The two are students at Oakland University in Rochester, but rent a house in Clawson. I have only met Stace a few times, but I work with Kelly every Monday, Wednesday, and Friday. Kelly is earning a degree in Women's Studies. When I asked her what she planned to do with her degree after she graduated, she told me she would continue selling housewares, but would have the credentials needed to be offended by how they were branded.

"How can you work on four hours of sleep?" I ask. I key in the safe code and sit back to wait the three minutes for it to open. "I didn't even do that when I was your age."

"You were a mother of two at my age. Speaking of, you're coming tonight, right?"

Kelly and her housemates are throwing a "we don't have air con-

ditioning and it's finally cool enough for us to invite people over"
party. She's been planning it for weeks, raiding the clearance section
for the last of the mismatched graduation party supplies.

"I don't know, Kell. It's been a long week."

"Hey! You said you'd come. The boys are with their dad—you
have no excuse."

"Aren't I a little old to be going to a college party?"

When the safe beeps, I pull out the tills and start counting the
cash in each one, checking the totals against the log from the night
before.

"Look, I know you think you're some old lady, but you're only
twenty-seven. Stace invited some nursing students that are your age."

I count the money out loud, waving my hand at her to get her to
stop talking. I am going to lose my place.

"I'm not going to stop talking until you say you'll come. Five.
Sixteen. Forty-seven. Twenty-three."

I record the till amount in the log, thrust the till into Kelly's
hands and say, "Fine. I'll come. Just shut up."

She smirks and starts toward the backroom door.

"Oh, and Kelly," I call after her. She turns. "Apparently a
tornado went through clearance last night. Can you start there?"

"Aww, shit."

§

I count out the second till and bring it to the front. As soon as
Shana arrives, I will have her start a register, but I know she will skirt
in at the last possible minute. When she does arrive, her white button-
down shirt is tucked into her belted khakis, her makeup is artfully
applied—no hair is out of place.

"Sorry I'm late," she says, which is her mantra. "Car wouldn't
start."

It is always 'Sorry-I'm-late-fill-in-the-blank.' She's sorry she's late
because she couldn't find her keys, because the alarm on her phone

didn't go off, because her cat got sick and puked in her shoe.

"No problem," I tell her. "You're on register two this morning—the till is already in there and counted."

Shana and Kelly used to date, which makes these Friday morning shifts when we all work together tense. Shana seems to be taking the break-up harder, and is inclined to sulk and get quiet when she and Kelly have to spend too much time together.

I have developed a system to keep everyone happy on these Fridays—Shana works the reg and Kelly stays on the floor, except when things get really busy, like during the eleven to one lunch rush. It works—Kelly is methodical and plows through tasks one at a time. The entire store will be cleaned and stocked and ready for the weekend before the night crew even arrives. Shana, on the other hand, is infinitely patient with the guests, whereas sometimes Kelly has to fight to keep her temper.

It's a good day—a steady stream of customers that almost never gets too heavy, which keeps Shana from becoming complacent, but allows Kelly to stay on the floor.

"Things got a little dicey at the end of the lunch rush," I say to Cindy, the closing shift manager. She is counting the tills for the night crew that will start to trickle in between 3:30 and 4 p.m. "The stupid registry kiosk went haywire again."

"What is with that thing?" Cindy says, popping her gum. She just got married over the summer, and the gigantic diamond on her left hand sparkles sharply in the fluorescent lights. "You know it pooped out last Saturday, and I spent the entire afternoon just running back and forth from the back printing out registries. Everyone was pissed off. Sucked."

"Well, the guy has already been out to fix it, and I was able to print a test one. I only had to print two from the back, but it was still a pain."

"How's everything else?" Cindy initials the logbook and closes the safe door. I help her carry the tills to the front of the store.

"Good. I had Kelly on the floor all day, so the place is restocked and spotless. You guys will probably need to hit candles, clearance, and frames before you go, but everything else should be set for tomorrow."

I think about mentioning how destroyed clearance was when I got in this morning, but decide against it. Cindy is nice, but she can get nasty when confronted head on—Vince gets paid the big bucks to deal with it, and I'm tired.

"Awesome," she says, closing the register drawer with her hip. "I love closing after you."

"Do me a favor and check me out?" I ask. I pull Mrs. Sawicki's cushion sets from behind the counter.

"That'll be $31.80," Cindy says after typing in my employee number. "Don't you live in an apartment?"

"Yeah—they're for my next door neighbor."

Kelly emerges from the back room. "You. My house. Eight o'clock," she says, shouldering her purse. She has a smear of dust across her cheek. I had her Windex the bathroom fixtures area—the yuck on some of the soap dishes was almost an inch thick. While I was wrapping a wedding shower gift, a large glass Mikasa platter that the bride hadn't registered for, I could hear Kelly sneezing, even over the guest explaining that her "nephew's fiancée registered for black dishes. Who's ever heard of black dishes?"

"I'll be there with mom jeans on," I say, walking out of the store after her.

I look back to see if Shana's heard our conversation—she is removing her apron and stuffing it into her purse, but judging by the way she is resolutely not looking in my and Kelly's direction, I guess that she's heard every word.

"You don't own mom jeans," Kelly says. She unlocks her car door and gets inside.

She's right. I joined the Barry Elementary School PTO while the boys were in preschool and first grade, but I got so sick of the nasty looks from the other, older mothers, that I only did it for one year—despite being an excellent ice cream social organizer.

"Hey!" I knock on Kelly's window, and she opens her car door. The power windows on her powder blue Lumina haven't worked in years. "What should I bring?"

"Seriously? It's a college party, Amb. If you don't like keg beer, bring whatever you like to drink."

"So don't bring a tray of deviled eggs?"

§

It's a little after 4 p.m., but already the sun is going down. It hasn't yet taken on that brittle quality Michigan sun gets in winter, and still cuts warmly through the chill air, gilding the leaves that have begun to change color but still cling tightly to their trees.

I always feel weird driving home on these Fridays. Every other day I would be rushing to pick David and Gary up from latchkey. There are a lot of kids that attend the Barry Elementary after-school program—their friends' mothers who don't have to work volunteer. They give the kids apple juice and carrot sticks, organize kick ball games, and even help Gary with his long division, which he is hating passionately. I figure it must run in the family—I hated long division, too.

But on every other Friday, Doug-the-ex-husband picks the boys up from school and keeps them for the weekend. Sometimes Kelly and I will get dinner or go out for drinks, but more often than not, I spend that time alone: cleaning up the house, doing the grocery shopping, and catching up on laundry from the week. Two little boys make a mountain of dirty clothes.

Mrs. Sawicki opens the door on my second knock. She has traded her pink nylon robe for a flower-printed house dress, the kind with pearlized snap buttons like my grandmother used to wear.

Where does she even buy this stuff?

I hold up the bag. "I have your seat cushions!"

Mrs. Sawicki opens the door, and the earthy smell of cooking cabbage and tomato sauce rushes out.

"Ah, you're too good to me," she says, taking the bag. "Come in. You hungry? I am making golumpkis to heat up tomorrow for lunch when Marcia is here. Stay for dinner."

I waver on the porch. When I don't have the boys to cook for, dinner usually degrades into a Stouffer's lasagna when I'm feeling industrious or chicken shawarma takeout when I'm not. My stomach rumbles.

"Golumpkis sound great," I say and follow Mrs. Sawicki inside.

The television in the corner is turned to the four o'clock news, a feature story about the hottest pet Halloween costumes.

"Costumes for dogs. What next?" She turns the television off.

I follow her into the kitchen, which is laid out exactly like mine, with a dinette set against the far wall. Mrs. Sawicki's table and chairs obviously aren't from Target—the Formica table is trimmed in chrome. The four matching chairs have chrome legs and are covered in mustard-colored vinyl cushions. On the wall over the table is a large framed photo of Mrs. Sawicki with a man, shot in the 1970s— Mrs. Sawicki's hair is pale blond and teased into a compact beehive, and she wears a voluminous pink blouse cuffed tightly at the wrists. Mr. Sawicki has thinning dark hair and a dark mustache, wearing a shirt the same shade as his wife's under a maroon polyester suit.

Mrs. Sawicki tears open the plastic on two of the cushion sets. One of the dinette chair's seats has been patched with duct tape, and Mrs. Sawicki covers it with the bright orange plastic cushion before inviting me to sit.

"Is that a picture of you and your husband?" I ask as she bustles around the kitchen, setting the table with paper napkins, spooning the steaming cabbage dumplings onto Corelle plates trimmed with brown flowers.

"Yes, that is my Oskar. We had that taken for our tenth wedding anniversary. Look at how young I was!"

I know her husband passed away several years ago. After my divorce, the boys and I moved into the complex, and I met Mrs. Sawicki's daughter, Marcia. She was shoveling and salting Mrs. Sawicki's walkway while I was scraping off my car for one of my rare Saturday shifts. I introduced myself, and Marcia explained that she was there caring for her mother, who had lived in the complex alone since her husband's death in the early nineties.

I want to ask Mrs. Sawicki how her husband died, but I don't know how, so I say instead, "I hope the boys didn't give you any trouble this morning."

"No, dear. They are good boys. So quiet and well behaved."

I snort, but the truth is, sometimes they are quiet. Eerily so. Just this morning, while Gary was packing his homework into his book bag, I was sitting with David at the kitchen table. We were both eating bowls of Honey Nut Cheerios, and David was staring out of the doorwall while he chewed.

"Mommy?" he said, turning his solemn eyes on me. They were brown, like his father's, and big for his little face. They were also perpetually ringed in dark circles.

"Yes, honey?"

"What would you do if me and Gary died?"

I was so startled that I breathed in a partially-chewed Cheerio and had to cough it up, scaring David so that his eyes grew enormous.

"What would make you ask a question like that?"

"It's just, who would take care of you? You and Daddy don't live together anymore. If me and Gary weren't here, you'd be all alone." David had abandoned his Cheerios, which were starting to bloat in his cereal bowl. His bottom lip trembled.

I knelt next to his chair and hugged him. "You're right. So I guess you and Gary better be extra careful to make sure nothing happens to my special guys."

Just then, Gary walked into the kitchen, a half-eaten Strawberry Pop Tart in one hand, his backpack in the other.

"What's going on?" he asked, spraying crumbs as he spoke.

"Nothing," I said over David's head. "Go put your shoes on."

§

Mrs. Sawicki pours me a glass of milk, and I try not to laugh—I haven't drunk milk with my dinner since I was eight years old.

"Well, I am sure they are a comfort to you," she says. "I miss hearing children's voices. My son John and his wife aren't able to have them, and I don't know if Marcia will ever get married. 'Ma,' she says, 'I have hundreds of furry children.' She's a vet, you know. How do you like the golumpkis?"

"Very good," I say, and begin cutting into my third cabbage roll. Doug's family is Polish, and his mother makes golumpkis—but they aren't as good as Mrs. Sawicki's. I always thought they were bland because they needed salt, but now I realize that they are bland because they lack any kind of spice. Mrs. Sawicki's tomato sauce is speckled with herbs, and I can taste herbs in the beef and rice filling, as well.

It has been years since I've eaten Doug's mother's cooking—when things between Doug and I started to go south, that was the first thing that went. Doug's family receded, we stopped attending holidays. In our final year together, the only time his mom and dad saw the kids was when Doug took them over on the weekends without me. The whole thing was so unnatural and dumb. It's easy to not miss it.

"Can I get you another one, dear?" Mrs. Sawicki asks, reaching for my dish.

I drink the last of my milk and wipe my mouth with my paper

napkin.

"No, thank you."

I can't believe I've eaten three of the big cabbage rolls. I hadn't eaten anything since my baked ziti Smart Ones at eleven this morning, and I was hungry. But the rice, beef, and milk sit heavy in my stomach.

"I should go," I say, rising. "A friend from work is having a small party tonight and invited me. I need to get ready."

"Thank you for keeping this old woman company," Mrs. Sawicki says. When she gets to her feet, both of her knees creak, and I remember that Gary once said Mrs. Sawicki sounded like his dad's house settling in the night. I'd chastised him, but he was right.

"Thank you for dinner. And as always, if you need anything, I am just next door."

"I know, dear. Thank you."

The stab of guilt I feel when I walk across the tiny yard to my own door is not unlike the guilt of leaving the boys at school in the morning.

§

I shower and stand dripping in a towel before my closet. It feels decadent—when the boys are home, showers are rushed affairs, and I always bring my clothes into the bathroom with me. I got a small raise when I was promoted to weekday manager, and I am hoping the extra money will be enough to afford a larger place. I'd love for Gary and David to have their own rooms, and I would really love to give the boys their own bathroom. A while ago, I stopped buying my shampoo—the boys' kids' shampoo is thick and bright green like slime. It makes my hair smell like watermelon bubble gum, but at least it's easy to comb.

"What should I even wear to this thing?"

I half-expect one of the boys to ask "What thing?" and feel lonely when no one answers back.

In the end, I choose a pair of dark jeans and a green-and-white striped sweater that Kelly complimented one night when we went for drinks. She asked me if I got it from Forever 21 and was amused when I told her it was older than my kids. I keep my makeup simple, just a little eye shadow and mascara, blow-dry my hair, and grab my canvas jacket before heading out the door.

It's full dark, but in the glare of the porch light, my breath billows in white plumes. It's definitely cold enough for an un-air conditioned house party.

§

Kelly and her roommates rent a house just off Main Street in Clawson, behind where the old Ambassador Skating Rink used to be. The neighborhood is a grid of streets, dilapidated houses with white or blue or yellow siding, spaced evenly apart and already decorated with carved pumpkins and fake spider webs.

Kelly's house is the most decorated one on the block. I recognize last year's Bed, Bath and Beyond products—purple house lights, those Jell-O-like window clings shaped like orange pumpkins, white ghosts, and black cats. There is also a giant pumpkin on the porch which someone has carved to look like the Joker's face from *The Dark Knight*.

From the street, I can hear music coming from inside, muffled, as if it is oozing out through ill-fitted window panes and the cracks around the door jamb. Stace answers the door when I knock.

"Amber!" she says, pulling me inside the house and shutting the door behind us. "I'm so glad to see you."

It's a strange greeting from someone I have only hung out with a couple of times. The hall is warm. I shed my jacket, but I can feel sweat gathering on my upper lip. "Thanks for inviting me."

"Yeah, Kelly bet me five bucks that you were going to wimp out and not come. Let's go collect."

I don't know what to say, so I say nothing, and instead follow

Stace through the front hall and into the kitchen. People I don't know, mostly women, are clumped in groups and talking loudly over the music. There's a keg in the corner next to a stack of white plastic cups printed with black graduation hats.

"You want a beer?" Without waiting for an answer, Stace weaves her way to the keg and starts pouring me one.

The too-foamy beer is one of the lights, either Bud or Miller, but at least it's cold. When I nod thanks, Stace continues through the kitchen into the dining room. The table, pushed against the wall, is covered in a paper cloth that matches the cups. The girls used plastic trick-or-treating buckets to hold regular potato chips and Kelly's beloved Cool Ranch Doritos. There's also salsa in a bowl shaped like a skull with the cranium removed, cheese cubes stabbed with cocktail swords, and, on the floor next to the table, a giant washtub filled with floating apples.

"Bobbing for apples?" I ask.

Stace shrugs. "It was Kelly's idea. She didn't want to do a costume party, but it's pretty much a Halloween party, anyway."

Kelly is kneeling in front of a laptop connected to the stereo, fiddling with the music selection. She's wearing a pair of tight jeans that cut into her sides and her tight black t-shirt is riding up.

"Amber's here. You owe me five bucks!"

Kelly gets to her feet, her chest and face red with alcohol. She puts her arms around Stace's waist and says, "I'm a little short on cash. Can I pay you in some other way?" Kelly leans in and kisses her girlfriend deeply, a closed-eyes open mouth kiss like in the movies. I feel uncomfortable, like I shouldn't be there, or they shouldn't be.

I've worked with Kelly for a few years. Gary and David call her Aunt Kell. We've hung out in bars, and once, we went to a sketchy dance club in Pontiac, but I've never seen this side of her. Even when we are talking about her relationships, she skirts the issue of sex.

When they disentangle, Kelly turns to me. "You having a good time?"

"Well, I just got here, so, you know, I haven't tongue-kissed anyone yet," I say.

Kelly smiles. "There's still time. Come on, I'll introduce you to some people from school."

All of Kelly's school mates are women, and I guess that most of them are also lesbians—girls with their arms around each other's waists, or standing with arms touching. There is one attractive couple wearing tank tops and jeans, their hands in each other's back pockets, like a black-and-white Calvin Klein ad.

The girls are discussing a feminist philosophy class they're all enrolled in. Apparently the instructor is having the students read a novel written by Mary Wollstonecraft, which half that group is pleased about, and the other half of the group doesn't like.

"I have nothing against the works of Wollstonecraft, of course. But why are we reading *Maria*? It's a philosophy course. We should be reading *A Vindication*."

"No way," pipes up one-half of the back-pocket couple. She is a diminutive blond with thin wrists and long fingers encircling her beer cup. "*Maria* weaves in all of Wollstonecraft's views of the British monarchy. I can't wait for Professor Jackson to pick it apart."

I drink my beer, enthralled. In some ways, it is exactly how I had imagined college parties—twenty-somethings standing around drinking keg beer and talking about the books they've read. I have nothing to add. But then, even if the conversation turned to movies or TV shows, I wouldn't be much more prepared—unless they watch *Phineas and Ferb* or have seen *The Croods* in the theater.

"Professor Jackson taught the feminist poetry class last Spring," Kelly says to me. She twinkles her fingers around her earlobes and I vaguely remember Kelly talking about one of the new professors in the department, who always wears long silver earrings that brush her shoulders and tinkle when she walks, but I can't remember if Kelly liked her or not—so I just nod my head and finish my beer.

"Can I get you another?" Kelly asks, reaching for my cup. She just misses it, grabs on to my sweater sleeve instead.

"Ah, sure." I place the cup in her fingers.

As she walks away, it's as if her friends suddenly notice I'm there.

"How do you know Kelly?" the blond with the delicate wrists asks me.

"We work together."

"At the hotline?"

I know that every other Saturday, Kelly volunteers for the Haven 24-hotline, taking calls from abused women. Stace volunteers there, too, which is how they met.

"No. We work together at Bed, Bath, and Beyond."

As soon as I say this, something changes—it isn't as tangible as a facial expression or a shift in posture, but it's something. Like the light suddenly dimming or the temperature ratcheting up.

"Don't you feel like all of those stores carry all the same stuff?" This is the girl that didn't want to read the Wollstonecraft novel.

I don't know what she means. Linens 'n' Things was our closest competitor, but they haven't had a brick and mortar store in years. I shrug.

"It's just, everyone buying all the same spoons, all the same teapots. Stores like Bed, Bath, and Beyond are contributing to the homogenization of America," the girl continues, her twenty-year-old face scornful. The other twenty-year-old faces all nod in agreement, and I get mad. It feels like a personal attack.

I want to ask, "How the hell should I know? I'm just a store manager!" or "So! What's so wrong with everyone owning the same spoons?" Instead, I say, "Well, Bed, Bath, and Beyond keeps my kids fed and gives me health insurance, so if that's what you mean by homogenization, then I guess, yeah, they do contribute to it."

That shuts them up. One of the group even gasps, but whether it is from my obvious anger or the mention of my kids, I don't know. Either way, I weave my way back to the kitchen, looking for Kelly. I want to tell her that her friends are jerks and that I'm leaving, but she is nowhere to be found.

I feel a hand on my arm, and turn to see a man holding a cup full of keg beer. He is one of only a handful of guys at the party.

He smiles. "Believe it or not, they didn't mean to be rude."

"Excuse me?"

"The girls back there. I couldn't help but overhear your conversation with them. They're okay so long as you don't take anything they say seriously. The name's Michael, by the way."

Michael looks as out of place as I feel—he has big, workman's hands speckled with freckles. His strawberry blond hair is short and he wears a tidy beard.

"I'm Amber," I say. The adrenaline has stopped pumping and I realize that I am sweating in earnest.

"Can I get you a drink?" Michael asks.

"Actually, I think I need some air."

Michael nods and leads the way—through the kitchen to the hallway and out the front door. The night air needles through the weave of my sweater, chilling all the places that have just been sweating. I take a deep breath.

"I was in class with a lot of those girls last semester. A few of them talk first and think second. It's easy to be in college and have opinions about things you don't understand," Michael says.

I am reminded of a few years ago, when I was still on the PTA of Gary and David's school. I was doing some dishes and watching the boys play in the backyard through the kitchen window. Out of nowhere, Gary smacked his brother upside the head with a wiffle ball bat. The bat was cheap plastic, and besides being stunned, David was unharmed—but the behavior was so disturbing that I dragged Gary inside the house, yelled, and then made him sit at the kitchen table until dinner.

He was furious, and I could see him get angrier as I ignored his harrumphing and chair leg kicking. Finally, Gary turned an imperious face to me and said, "Don't you think you're over-compensating because you're a young mother?"

I had been in the middle of coating chicken tenders in crushed corn flakes prior to baking when I paused, the tender in my hand dripping egg wash back into the bowl.

"What did you say to me?" I asked. I could feel my pulse beating in my throat. I watched Gary go still, eyes large, realizing that he'd made a mistake.

"Nothing," he mumbled.

"That's what I thought. Now shut up until I say you can move."

I knew Gary was only repeating something he'd heard from one of his friends' mothers, or from one of the women that volunteered in the lunch room. And as the chill evening air cools the sweat from my face, it is clear that the girls from the Wollstonecraft conversation are no different—repeating something that they heard someone else say in order to sound smart.

Michael pulls a crumpled pack of cigarettes from his shirt pocket and offers it to me. I shake my head and try not to smile. He smokes cloves.

"So, you took classes with those girls? Does that mean you're a Women's Studies major?" I ask.

"English," he says and lights one of his cigarettes with a plastic lighter. In its flickering light, the shadows in the hollows of Michael's eyes deepen, making him appear, momentarily, ancient. "I took feminist poetry to meet girls."

For the first time the whole night, I laugh. "How's that working out for you?"

"Well, most of the girls in the class were ALSO interested in meeting girls—but it was okay. Kelly's cool, and I like most of her friends. And the professor was interesting—she focused a lot on the history surrounding the work." Michael blows the smoke away from where we're standing, but I can still smell it—like smoking a cigarette made of cotton candy.

"Sounds interesting," I say.

"You go to Oakland?"

I shake my head. "I'm not in school."

"Is that because of your kids?" Michael asks. He takes a seat on the porch steps, the wood creaking under his weight. I pull my jacket on and sit beside him.

"Sort of. I got married right after graduation and we started a family right away."

"You're married?"

"Divorced."

Inside the house, the music changes—the song is quieter but familiar, and I strain to listen. It's Radiohead, a band I first heard when I was in high school, while driving around in Doug's mom's Taurus, going to football games or staying out until 4 a.m., drinking coffee at Ram's Horn. Before David and Gary. Before I needed Doug to be anything except present.

"I love this song," I say.

Michael turns towards the door, trying to listen. "What is it?" he asks.

"'Creep.'"

"I don't know it."

Of course he doesn't—the song's twenty years old at least.

A gust of wind blows down the street, picking up leaves, yellow and brown, and plastering them against cars and the sides of houses. I feel old and tired.

The song ends, replaced by something louder that is completely foreign. "Yeah, I should go," I say, rising to my feet. "If you see Kelly, will you tell her thanks for me?"

Michael gets to his feet, too. "Is it your kids?"

"They're with their dad this weekend, but, I just need to go." I start down the steps, heading for my car.

"Would you like to go get a cup of coffee or something somewhere?"

I think of those cups of Ram's Horn coffee and almost smile. The Ram's Horn isn't even there anymore. "I don't think so."

"Well, can I call you sometime?"

I stop on the sidewalk and turn back. The conversation feels foreign, like watching a movie I have never seen before. I am trying to figure out Michael's angle. "Why?"

Michael's features are dim and blurred in the purple glow of the houselights, but I think he looks sheepish. "Because you're pretty."

That's not what I was expecting. It's been awhile since someone has called me pretty. "I'm old enough to be your mom."

"How old are you?"

"Twenty-seven."

Michael flicks his cigarette away and walks down the steps. "My parents are way older than you. They're at least thirty-two."

My stomach lurches, which must show on my face, because he quickly adds, "Hey, I'm kidding. My mom would have been ten years old when I was born. Look—you're nice. I like you. Let me take you out sometime."

"I don't know."

"I've got an idea. Just wait here a minute, okay? Don't leave yet."

When I nod, Michael turns and races down the sidewalk in the opposite direction. I watch as he unlocks a car a few houses down, rummages around in the front seat, and then jogs back to where I am standing. In his hand is a scuffed jewel case, which he gives to me.

"What is this?"

"It's a band I like called Of Monsters and Men. I stuck my number inside, so you don't have to feel pressured. You can listen to this CD, then ask Kelly about me, and once you're convinced that I'm a pretty great guy, you can call. Okay?"

"What if this music stinks, or Kelly tells me you're a jerk?"

"Then you can use it as a coaster. But you shouldn't. It's a good CD. And you should call me." With one last smile, Michael walks back toward the house.

Frost glitters on my windshield, and as I wait for the car to warm and melt it, I put Michael's CD in the player. The band is nothing like Radiohead—tempo sped up, hopeful instead of mournful. I realize as I pull onto Main Street that I have already decided to ask Kelly about her friend Michael when I see her at work on Monday.

I take the slow way home, through Clawson into Troy. I have the window rolled down—it's so cold that it makes my hands ache, but I enjoy the sound the rushing wind makes, and the crisp smell of autumn carried with it. I think about next weekend, when I'll have the boys at home with me. Maybe there will be enough leaves in the yard to rake into piles that the boys can jump in.

When I pull into the driveway, I can see that Mrs. Sawicki's house is dark. My own front window looks bright in comparison, from David's hall light, which he assures me he no longer needs but won't let me unplug. The yellow glow, spilling out onto the front lawn, looks warm and reassuring.

Orderly

When Janice found Shane, he was eating dinner alone in the New Haven Medicomplex's employee lounge—a small, windowless room off the kitchen. The florescent light gave Shane's skin a yellowish cast and his eyes were the dark sockets of a skull. The supernaturally green chives covering his Wendy's baked potato looked like moss growing over a rock.

Janice's brown heels clicked across the tile floor, causing Shane to look up from his meal. The whipped butter was already melting through the chives and Shane had given up trying to open the sour cream container with his hands in favor of applying his teeth.

"There are kitchen shears in a utility drawer next to the ovens," Janice said.

Shane finally ripped the container open and squeezed the bright white sour cream onto his baked potato. "I have all the tools I need. Why you still here?" Shane pulled his phone out of his pocket and checked the time. "It's after nine, Jan."

Janice was one of the social workers at New Haven, but she also performed many of the administrative duties. Unlike Shane and the other members of the Care Team, she was usually able to keep more-normal hours.

"I had some work to finish up—and I wanted to talk to you."

Janice didn't sit; instead, she stood with her arms crossed.

"Uh oh." Shane gave up trying to carve into his baked potato with the flimsy plastic fork and knife, folded his hands, and looked expectantly up at Janice. "Is there a problem?"

She sighed. "Mrs. Michaels was admitted to the hospital this morning. She had a persistent cough and was wheezing."

"Pneumonia?" Shane asked. The youngest residents at New Haven were in their seventies, and Mrs. Michaels was not one of the youngest. Pneumonia could be a death sentence.

"That's what we thought, until we ran all the standard diagnostics, and her blood tested positive for THC."

§

For the residents of the New Haven Medicomplex, nine o'clock was lights out. The residents didn't have to go to sleep—they could watch television quietly in their rooms—but they were not allowed in the common areas or to roam the halls.

As the Care Team's night shift supervisor, it was Shane's job to walk the halls at ten to nine—to help wheel-chair-bound residents into bed, to ensure that everyone had taken his or her evening doses of medication, to see that everyone was comfortable and quiet for the night. Shane then took a half-hour break for lunch, usually chili, or a baked potato, or a six-piece chicken nuggets off of the Dollar Menu at the Wendy's next to New Haven. The final two hours of his shift were spent helping the overnight medic with inventory, joking with Ruby, the overnight receptionist, and rewalking the halls, ears tuned to the sounds of potential emergencies.

The soles of his black Dansko nursing shoes, a ridiculously-overpriced gift from his mother when he was promoted to night shift supervisor, allowed him to tread the institutional-brown carpet of New Haven soundlessly. He could feel, rather than hear, the electricity of the place—ventilators, humidifiers, monitors of all types, and the ever-present fizz of televisions playing low.

Despite his silence, and the thick quiet of unheard noises, Mrs. Michaels always seemed to know when Shane passed.

"Hello, Shane," she would call from her room. He could hear it, muffled but distinct, through the beige-painted steel door.

On nights when his hall check was rushed, when there was a mess that needed cleaning, or a resident needed to be taken to the hospital wing, Shane passed Mrs. Michaels' door without stopping. But on quiet nights, when he could walk the halls in a more-leisurely way, he would stop, poke his head in, and say hello.

On this particular night, Mrs. Michaels sat propped up in bed, the room dark except for the yellow glow of a bedside lamp. The television was off.

"You're not sleeping tonight, Mrs. Michaels?" Shane asked.

"Not tonight, dear," she said.

Shane stepped into the room and shut the door quietly behind him. The residents' rooms were more like dormitories—an open space with a hospital bed dominating a corner, a small sitting area with a television on a lazy susan so it could easily face the settee or the bed, and a small private bathroom. Most rooms, including Mrs. Michaels', also had a small refrigerator and microwave, but no full kitchen or stove, as all residents were required to eat their meals in the dining room. Shane wondered if the residents knew that the rooms were really designed for the New Haven employees, to allow them to easily move beds in and out, to transfer sick residents into the hospital wing and, more often than not, to replace the bed when the resident couldn't return to his or her room.

"Can I turn the television on for you? Make you a cup of tea?" Shane asked.

"No, thank you. But if you have a minute, would you stay and talk to an old woman?"

Shane checked his cell phone—it was just after eleven. It had been a quiet night, and he doubted Ruby or John, the overnight medic, would miss him for a few minutes.

Shane sat in the chair next to Mrs. Michaels' bed. Her room had the same brown carpeting as the hallway, the same beige-painted walls, and smelled like the antiseptic spray the cleaning crew used in the bathrooms and a musty, flowery smell, like dust on rose petals. The white institutional bed linens were covered with a hand-knitted afghan in shades of pink and orange.

"What shall we talk about?" Shane asked.

"You know, when I was your age or a bit younger, I was living in Greenwich Village in the mid 1950s."

"New York? How did you end up in Michigan?"

"I met my Raymond, settled down. We moved out here so he could take a job at the Rouge Tool & Die Works in Dearborn."

"What was New York like in the 1950s?" Shane asked. Sometimes, he forgot that the residents were more than just elderly people needing help with bathing, with getting in and out of bed—they were elderly people who had lived whole lives that he knew nothing about.

"Exciting. I was working as an artists' model, if you can believe it."

"You mean, like, naked?"

"Yes, dear," Mrs. Michaels said, grinning. "It was art. And the artists I worked with knew writers and musicians. I met Alan Ginsberg at the White Horse Tavern. Do you know who that is? He was a poet, but he's dead, I think."

"I know of him," Shane said. "He was one of the characters in *On The Road*, my favorite book in high school." After reading the book the first time, Shane had researched the real lives of all the characters, and then reread the book, trying to reconcile the facts with the fiction.

"There is something of a Sal Paradise in you, I think," Mrs. Michaels said.

"You read that book, too?"

"A long time ago. In the middle of the night, actually. Even when I was young, I had a hard time sleeping. The best sleep I ever had was during my time in Greenwich Village, after I smoked a marijuana cigarette."

Had she said, "After I was abducted by aliens," Shane wouldn't have been more surprised.

Mrs. Michaels continued, "I thought, 'You're young. Maybe you know where I could get some?'"

"You want to smoke pot?" Shane wondered if he had heard her correctly. The entire conversation was surreal, taking place in an old lady's dimly lit room in the middle of the night. Shane shook his head.

"Yes, please." Mrs. Michaels folded her hands primly in her lap.

Shane's own hand crept to his right pants pocket, where he kept his stash, one joint safely ensconced in a Celestial Seasonings collectable tin with the Sleepytime Tea bear dozing on the lid.

"You really think smoking a 'marijuana cigarette' will help you sleep?" Shane asked.

The old woman shrugged, her shoulders boney beneath her nightgown. "It might, and I am willing to try anything. It's tiresome, being awake at night when everyone else is asleep. When my Raymond was here with me, he would sometimes stay awake, too, which helped the time go more quickly. Every year since he passed, the nights seem to get longer and more quiet."

Shane held his breath for a moment and thought—if he got caught, he'd be canned for sure. But he looked again at Mrs. Michaels—even in the golden light of her nightstand lamp, her skin looked thin and bluish, her fingers brittle, the area around her eyes red. Shane made up his mind and exhaled.

"Okay, Mrs. Michaels. Get your coat."

§

"Is Mrs. Michaels all right?" Shane asked, worry twisting up his insides. He tried not to squirm.

"Aside from that big red flag, there isn't a thing wrong with her, which is how she became my problem," Janice said.

"You sure she didn't just eat some poppy seeds or something?"

"Nice try, smart guy. The only thing that has THC in it is dope, and after talking with her for twenty minutes, she finally admitted to smoking some with you."

"She said 'dope'?" Shane asked and snorted. He couldn't help it—the thought of an eighty-plus-year-old Mrs. Michaels saying "dope" was ridiculous.

Janice's brow unfurrowed and she smirked. "No. She said marijuana cigarettes."

"Am I fired?"

"You probably should be!" Janice sat in the chair across from Shane, releasing some of the tension from the room. "What on Earth were you thinking?"

"A month or so ago she told me she couldn't sleep, and when she couldn't sleep in the past, smoking a little pot helped. She didn't smoke much and I was with her the whole time. I didn't plan it. And I didn't sell it to her."

"If I thought you were pushing on the residents we wouldn't be having this conversation," Janice said sharply. She removed her wire-rimmed glasses and rubbed her eyes. Janice was of an indeterminate age—the grey threaded through her brown hair and the lines around her eyes and on her brow looked like they had been taken from an older woman and put on her face. Shane assumed being a social worker of any kind couldn't be easy, but it was especially difficult when your clients were certain to die before too long.

"Why are we having this conversation?" Shane asked after Janice replaced her glasses.

"Look, our residents—they're old. Everyone knows they're here until they die. We just try to make it as comfortable and enjoyable for them as we can. And you're good with them, Shane. They like you—not just Mrs. Michaels. And what she told you, about not sleeping, is true. When it was clear that her insomnia was chronic, we tried giving her a sedative at night—she slept a little, but it made her like a dementia patient during the day. She didn't know what was going on, and one day, she took a nasty tumble out of bed, so we took her off of it. But not sleeping isn't good—I was worried she'd end up in the psych ward."

"I had no idea," Shane said.

Janice shrugged. "It's more common than you'd think. But she says, with your 'help,' she's been sleeping. She's put on some weight, too."

Shane smiled.

"Slow down, hero. It's still totally illegal. Just, let me know, okay? Our residents are on a cocktail of medications. If I know about any 'self-medicating' they're doing, I can check their history and make sure the dope isn't going to interact with anything. Had this fallen on the other social worker's desk, you wouldn't only be fired, they'd throw your ass in jail."

Shane nodded. "Thanks, Janice."

She got to her feet. "Since I'm doing you a solid, will you return the favor and work a swing tomorrow? Carin's still not feeling right, and I don't want her around the residents if she's even a little sick."

He groaned. "That means I'm gonna have to be back here at 10 a.m."

"You can come in at 11."

Shane nodded. "I guess I owe you one."

"Thanks."

"And Jan, you'll want to check out Mr. Ramone's medications, too."

Janice turned to him, her eyes large.

Shane tried not to laugh. "It was only once or twice, but you said to let you know."

"I did say that, didn't I? Do me a favor and let's save all other surprises for tomorrow."

§

As Shane was walking to his car, his phone started vibrating in his pocket. It was a text from his mother:

HI HONEY WHEN ARE YOU WORKING A DAY SHIFT NEXT

Which meant she stayed up until after midnight to make sure he got it when he was getting off work.

Every time he had dinner with his folks he was subject to their passive aggressive disapproval of his decision not to go to college, which usually took the form of anecdotes about the great lives the people he knew from high school were leading. His mother was still friends with the other band booster moms and got her information at their monthly coffee dates.

When he'd had dinner at his parents' house two weeks before, his mother started in even before all the dishes had been passed. "I saw Tara's mom the other day—she loves being on Michigan State's color guard."

Shane was thankful that his mouth was full of meatloaf and mashed potatoes, because he could grunt an acknowledgement.

He heaped salad on his plate as his mother continued, "Apparently, she's been seeing State's drum major for a while now. I didn't realize that was a 'type.'"

Shane had been Troy High's drum major his senior year. When he took Tara to prom, she told him that she loved him, that Lansing was only an hour and a half from Troy. She said they'd make it work, and they did, until she came home for Thanksgiving and informed him that he was a loser with no ambition. They hadn't spoken since.

"And Bobby is doing well at Central. Even with his band duties his mother says that he got four As and one B+ last semester."

Shane swallowed what was in his mouth and took a drink of water. "You know, Mom, I don't really talk to any of those people anymore." He could feel his heart pumping in his throat, but he tried to seem unruffled.

"I know, Sweetie. I just thought you'd be interested in hearing the news, especially since their lives are so different from yours."

His mother was right about one thing—Shane's life was different from the lives of the people who used to be his best friends. Shane believed his decision to not go to school was practical—he didn't know what he wanted to do with the rest of his life, and he wasn't interested in spending $20,000 a year trying to figure it out. For whatever reason, his parents didn't get that, and the more his mother pushed, the more obstinate he felt.

There were days, when work was rough, when he was changing soiled bed linens, when the residents were cranky and bored, or worse, when he'd lost one, that Shane would wonder if he was making the right decision. Had he just done what his parents asked, he could be worried about an economics final or being too hung over to play trumpet in the marching band's half time show, instead of worrying about his charges dying.

But when his mother asked, "Have you given any more thought to picking up some classes at Oakland Community College? Now that you're working nights, you could enroll in day classes no problem."

Shane gritted his teeth, swallowed his mouth full of salad, and said, "Not really, no," with a smile.

He knew that if he went to dinner after his swing shift the next night, it would be more of the same. But he also knew that his mother would buy him a loaf of bread, a package of bologna, two boxes of cereal, milk, eggs. She always bribed him with groceries.

Shane dug his wallet out of his back pocket and saw he had thirteen dollars to last him until payday. If he had dinner at his folks', he could forgo the Dollar Menu and use that money to get another dime bag from Sarah.

So he texted back:

Tomorrow. Will be there round 6.

He set his phone on the car's hood as he rummaged through the pockets of his cargo pants in search of keys. A second text message sounded like thunder and almost sent the phone skittering over the edge. Shane assumed it was his mother responding, but instead it was a two word text from Margaret:

You coming?

§

The Cavalier groaned to life, the heavy guitar of early Smashing Pumpkins rattling the car's frame—Shane imagined the music shaking loose the rust crawling up the door from its bottom edge. Despite the fact that he was dead tired and had to be back at work in less than twelve hours, he threw the car into drive and headed for Ram's Horn, where the guys would be waiting. Margaret, Sarah, and Dennis were Shane's fellow "incompetent members of society," which was Sarah's term. Shane thought Sarah had the right to name their band of friends because she was the one who brought them all together.

The summer after Shane's senior year had been like any other, but fall came, everyone moved on to Michigan State, to Central, to U of M. Shane started work at New Haven and soon found himself very alone.

He'd known Sarah in high school tangentially—she hadn't been in band, but she dated one of the guys on the drumline for a while, and Shane got accustomed to seeing her gypsy skirts, handkerchief tops, and dreadlocks. Like the rest of the kids who smoked, he soon learned that Sarah was the best person to buy from because her folks grew it in their basement and dried it themselves.

As soon as he could afford it on his orderly salary, Shane moved out of his parents' house, got a grotty studio apartment in Sterling Heights right off the expressway, and called Sarah to make a buy. She told him then that she'd be at Ram's Horn for most of the night and to stop in there.

Two years later, the scene hadn't changed much—Sarah held court in one of the back booths, smoke from her menthols hazing the air of the 24 hour restaurant. Next to her sat Dennis, stocky with a blond crew cut. He'd been an "auto shop guy" in high school, but was now enrolled at OCC on the two-year firefighter track. Shane wasn't sure how Sarah knew him, but suspected that they'd dated for a while in the past. Across from Dennis was Margaret, Sarah's friend from way back and the only one of them that belonged in college. Shane didn't know all the details, but Sarah told him that Margaret had gotten into some school in Missouri known for its writing program, but half way through the first semester, she wigged and had to return home. Since then, the doctors were constantly changing her medication cocktail with varying results.

Just inside the Ram's Horn door was a glass refrigerator case, its naked florescent bulbs illuminating slices of coconut crème pie in sunken plastic wrap and sundae glasses filled with red Jell-O crowned with stiff-looking whipped topping. They rotated endlessly, the motor's hum harmonizing with the "Soft rock favorites of yesterday and today" playing quietly on the sound system.

"Long night?" Sarah asked when she saw him.

Margaret scooted over and Shane sank into the seat next to her.

"You could say that," he said, rubbing his eyes.

"Glad you came anyway," Margaret said.

"You want coffee?" Sarah waved to the waitress behind the front counter, the bracelets on her arm clinking musically.

"Unleaded. I gotta work a swing tomorrow, so I can't stay."

The waitress, fifty-year-old single mom Betty who was also friends with Sarah, placed the white ceramic decaf mug before him, filled it, then Sarah's and Dennis's brown mugs. With her latest round of medications, Margaret couldn't drink coffee—she said even decaf gave her the whim whams. She drank cups of hot chocolate instead, the whipped topping always melting over the side, and maybe it was that habit, or the medication itself, that had caused her to gain fifteen pounds.

Some nights, Shane would sit with the guys for hours, drinking bottomless cups of coffee, bumming Sarah's smokes or fries, and talking in a way that made him realize that he never really knew any of the people he was closest to while he was still in high school.

"You want to order food?" Betty asked him.

"No, thanks. Coffee's great."

As she walked away, Shane turned to Sarah and said low, "Actually, I gotta buy a dime bag with my last ten."

"I don't have anything with me, but I can swing by your place tomorrow night after I close the store."

Besides the small-time basement marijuana operation, Sarah's folks also owned Spirit Animal, a crystals and incense shop in south Troy. Despite the obvious conclusions that could be drawn, Sarah's folks kept their two businesses completely separate.

"It's pretty granola-y, but they really care about their customers' metaphysical health," Sarah said when Shane pointed out the ways in which the two businesses could lucratively overlap. "I don't know how much I buy into all of that, but I do think there is enough bad shit in this world that everyone can use all the help they can get."

"You still need the senior discount?" Sarah asked, grinning. When Shane started increasing his buying from once every couple of months to monthly-like-clockwork, Sarah asked about the uptick in consumption, and Shane told her about Mrs. Michaels. Since then, Sarah's folks had been more generous with how they weighed the bags.

"Can you guys not talk about this stuff in front of me?" Dennis asked. He'd been looking uncomfortable, shifting from one butt cheek to the other, and Shane wondered if he'd blow.

"Jesus, Dennis. You know we smoke," Sarah said, grinding out her menthol cigarette for emphasis. "I'm probably high right now."

Shane pointed to the plate of half-eaten chili fries, topped with onions and hardening cheese, in front of Sarah and asked, "Probably?"

Sarah stuck out her tongue, lifted the plate and offered him a cold fry. He took three.

"Dennis is right," Shane said around the chili. "He's going to be a public servant soon enough. We should at least pretend to be law-abiding citizens when we're around him. It's only polite. How're classes, by the way?"

"Hard," Dennis said. "I don't think I appreciated the amount of emergency health care I have to be ready to administer."

"You've been a volunteer firefighter for two years," Margaret said, draining her hot chocolate. Shane thought it was cute that Margaret's favorite part was the very last drop, the gritty chocolate silt.

"Yeah, but I can count on two hands the number of fires I have actually helped put out. It's not like we live in Detroit. Last week, I had to watch this video of real life emergency respondents—we're talking burned up bodies. One guy's head was taken clean off."

Margaret gasped but Sarah snickered and said, "I would guess there's not much you can do for a guy who's totally lost his head."

"Can you handle that?" Margaret asked.

Dennis shrugged. "I hope so. After the video, the instructor, an old guy who used to be a fire chief, said that he's seen a lot of guys get messed up after dealing with that stuff. He also said a lot of marriages don't last because of it, guys can't process what they see on the job and get withdrawn, start drinking, whatever."

"I don't think I could do it, man," Shane said, drinking his coffee. Ram's Horn went through so much coffee, even at night, that it never had the bitter, baked-taste like the coffee at work.

"You're around death all the time," Margaret said, nudging him.

"It's not the same—the residents are old. The only time I see it is when they've gone in their sleep, which is the quietest thing in the world. Any violent deaths take place in the hospital wing."

"Can you give Dennis one of these?" Margaret fished a leather thong out from inside her shirt. A black pointed crystal wrapped in silver wire hung off the end.

"Black tourmaline wouldn't be good for Dennis," Sarah said seriously. "But I can get you a piece of chrysoprase, which helps you be ready for action and encourages a positive outlook on life. I can sew it into the inside of your uniform."

Dennis smiled. "I'll take it."

"Sarah said this is for protection and logical thinking. She just got it for me," Margaret said, holding the crystal out to Shane. He inspected it, the diffuse-light from the green pendant lamps making it look impenetrably black. He shifted his eyes to Sarah, who was looking at Margaret intently, forehead creased in worry, and he guessed that Margaret's latest round of medications weren't working.

"It feels nice in the hand, doesn't it?" Shane said, running his thumb over the crystal before giving it back.

"Did you know that when you rub black tourmaline it becomes charged with energy?" Sarah asked through a snicker, herself again.

"Where do you get this stuff?" Dennis asked.

"My mom got on a 'professional development' kick and made me read *Healing Crystals and Gemstones: From Amethyst to Zircon*. Now I can help customers find the kind of healing they need."

"That's a thing?" Shane asked.

"It was pretty interesting. Not sure how much I believe it, but a hunk of quartz is cheaper than going to a doctor—$2.99, to be exact."

"What would you prescribe for Shane?" Margaret asked, bumping him again. She was sweating slightly in the warm restaurant, and Shane could smell her perfume, like roses and something sweeter.

Sarah thought a moment, then said, "Garnet."

"What's it do?" Dennis asked.

"It will help Shane find what he's looking for." The gravity with which Sarah spoke made the hairs on the back of Shane's neck stand on end.

§

Shane begged off as soon as his coffee was done and Margaret offered to walk him to his car. She slipped her hand into his before they passed the refrigerated dessert case, and Shane was reminded of the week before, when he'd watched Margaret leave the restaurant only after being coaxed from the bathroom by her mother.

Shane had met Margaret, Sarah, and Dennis after work. Shane had just been paid, and was relishing a BLT sandwich and a pile of french fries drowning in catsup.

The four of them were having a discussion on the morality of old folks homes—Sarah's grandmother, who was almost eighty and still living on her own, fell on the sidewalk while dragging a bag of leaves to the curb and broke her arm. When Sarah's hippie parents started talking about living options for Grandma, Sarah called them both selfish jerks and left the house.

"I'm just saying, people shouldn't be allowed to just abandon their family members in some industrialized mausoleum until they die. It should be illegal," Sarah said.

When Sarah took a drag off her cigarette, Shane could see her hand shake. Dennis must have seen it, too, because he moved Sarah's half-full coffee cup to the middle of the table and said, "When Betty comes back around, I'm having her switch you to decaf."

"You're not being fair, about the mausoleum thing," Shane said. "I mean, I've seen the news, and I know some old folks homes are bad, but New Haven's not like that. In most cases, our residents are there because they can't take care of themselves, and their families can't care for them, either. But they're not abandoned. I know a lot of the residents' families."

"But even you say you feel like a prison guard sometimes," Dennis said.

"Only when a fight breaks out." Shane had already told them the story of how two residents got into a fight over what to watch on the big screen television in the common area. It was mostly just shoving, but a pair of dentures was dropped and damaged in the scuffle, and both residents had to be escorted back to their rooms.

"Any place can feel like prison if you're trapped there long enough."

When Margaret spoke, the three of them turned to look at her. Shane knew Margaret's prison comment was about being home all the time. She didn't talk about missing school, but when she wasn't feeling well, she would talk about how her parents 'keep her locked up' and 'never let her see the sun.'

"You feeling all right, honey?" Sarah asked.

"Haven't been sleeping. I'm fine. Don't look at me."

Shane, who was sitting across from Sarah, watched Sarah go instantly still. Dennis, seated next to Sarah, just looked confused.

"What part of 'stop looking at me' don't you understand?" Margaret asked Dennis directly.

"I wasn't looking at you," he said. Dennis made eye contact with Shane, looking for corroboration. Shane shook his head slightly.

"Well, I'm sorry, *Dennis*, if I make you uncomfortable. But *you're* the one wearing a brown shirt. We can all see that." Margaret's voice had gotten louder, and the other patrons in the sleepy, nighttime restaurant stopped their conversations to watch the booth.

"Margaret, you're not making any sense," Dennis said, his voice low. "Want us to call your folks for you?"

Sarah unfroze and punched Dennis in the arm. Out of the corner of his eye, Shane could see Margaret's face turn crimson.

"Don't you dare call those people," Margaret shouted. She got up out of the booth and started to walk around the restaurant.

"Honey, come back to your seat," Sarah said coaxingly, but turned daggers on Dennis, who already looked like he wished the terra cotta tiles with black grout would open up and swallow him.

When Margaret walked to the other end of the restaurant and sat down at another couple's table, Sarah scrambled over Dennis to follow her, trailing one of her scarves into Shane's catsup and upsetting her tepid coffee, which made a caramel-colored waterfall off the end of the table.

Margaret was talking animatedly and angrily at the startled couple. "We're all prisoners here. Like butterflies, impaled with giant pearl-headed pins, flapping our wings uselessly under glass. Just try to leave. Just try it!"

Margaret picked up the woman's fork out of a plate of scrambled eggs with toast, but before she could do anything with it, Sarah had grabbed her other hand and was pulling her away from the booth. Shane watched as Sarah rubbed her hands over Margaret's arms, as if to warm her. He saw Sarah's lips move as she spoke low, but was too far away to hear what was being said. When Sarah tried to touch Margaret's hair, Margaret dropped the fork loudly, shouted "Just leave me alone!" and ran into the bathroom.

Sarah ran back to the booth, grabbed her bag from the corner, and called Margaret's parents. It was 1 a.m.

When they arrived, Margaret's mother talked Margaret out of the bathroom while Margaret's father paid for the couple's bill and apologized for his daughter's "interruption." Sarah hovered near, ready to offer support if she could, but Shane and Dennis sat helpless in the booth, watching events unfold with the rest of the restaurant patrons and staff.

"Can I pay your bill?" Mr. Rogers asked Sarah while they waited.

"No," Sarah said, looking back at the table, a row of soggy

napkins damming the coffee waterfall. "Dennis is buying our dinners tonight."

There was the sound of a door crashing against a wall and Margaret appeared. Without looking at anyone, she marched across the restaurant and out of the back door. Mrs. Rogers followed behind, the circles under her eyes stark in her pale face. The silver threading her dark hair glinted when she got close to the dessert case. Mrs. Rogers pulled Sarah into a quick, fierce hug before following Margaret. She looked once at where Shane and Dennis were sitting, mouthed "Thank you" before leaving the restaurant. Shane thought that if the ground would oblige Dennis by opening up, he might jump into the abyss, too.

Even though Margaret still wasn't wholly herself, Shane was grateful that she was more here than not, and gave her hand a squeeze.

"You were pretty quiet tonight," Margaret said.

"Nothing gets by you, does it?"

"It's my gift. But no changing the subject. Did something happen at work?"

Shane thought about making an excuse for his reticence—he was tired, he had to have dinner with his folks the next night—but he decided against it. Shane suspected that everyone in Margaret's life—her folks, Sarah, other friends—surrounded her with a sea of eggshells. He couldn't be sure, but Shane wondered if their careful ministrations just made things worse for her.

"One of the social workers found out about Mrs. Michaels and her marijuana cigarettes," he finally said.

"Shit. Did you get in trouble?"

He smirked. "No. If I was working at any other old age home, or if this had come across the desk of anyone else, I'd probably be in jail. But I guess Janice and I think alike."

"In what way?"

"It's like, my job is to help people limp the last few steps to death. There's nothing I can do about it. I can't stop it from happening. But every once in a while, I can help the residents remember they're still alive. Like Mrs. Michaels and the pot. Or, because so many of our residents are diabetic, they only serve sugar free Jell-O and pudding in the caf, so when I worked mid shifts, I would sneak this one old dude with a sweet tooth Frostys. Stupid stuff. But it feels like it's all they got."

"I don't think it's stupid," Margaret said. "Sarah and Dennis wouldn't, either."

"Yeah, but I didn't want Sarah to start on 'This is why pot should be legal,' which only annoys Dennis. I just wanted everyone to be happy tonight. We can change the world tomorrow."

The late September air was full of cold mist, obscuring the streetlamps illuminating the parking lot. He zipped up his black hoodie and noticed that Margaret was just standing in a t-shirt.

"You should go back in. Aren't you cold?" Shane asked. He put his hands on her bare forearms, but they were warm like the maroon-rubber water bottles some of the residents used at night.

"No. I think it's this new medicine."

"Has it been helping?"

"What's 'helping?' I have these weird dreams where I'm flying and the world below me looks like a smeary Monet painting. I sweat all the time. I can't tell you if that makes me better."

"Have you told your folks?"

Margaret shook her arms loose, walked around the car once. Shane stood still, willing Margaret to settle. When she finally wandered back to him, Shane could see that her eyes glinted with what Sarah called her "manic fire."

"Sorry," Margaret said, and took a few measured breaths. "It's just, my folks are so scared. I don't know what the hell they have to be so afraid of. I'm the one who's crazy. I take meds that make me fat or make it so I can't sleep or concentrate or write. But when I tell them that the meds make it worse, they freeze up. I am pretty sure my mom thinks that if she holds her breath long enough, I'll turn uncrazy."

"Hey," Shane said, moving slowly, grabbing onto Margaret's hands, which quivered.

"Don't tell me to calm down," she said, her voice low.

"Do I look stupid?"

She smiled. "Your shoes look a little stupid."

"You're not crazy. If there's one thing I've learned from working at New Haven, it's that crazy is not like people think it is. Maybe you have a chemical thing. Maybe you need more sleep. Maybe you need to talk to someone. That doesn't make you crazy. And you're not fat."

"I can't stop eating sweets. I had to buy all new pants."

A lock of brown hair had tumbled loose from Margaret's ponytail. Shane brushed his fingers across her forehead and tucked the lock behind her ear, which made her smile again.

"Well, when you smile now, you have these two really cute dimples that you used to hide before, so I guess I'm all for new pants."

Margaret leaned her head against his chest. "Are you sure you don't want a girlfriend?" she said into his hoodie.

He kissed the top of her head. "Sometimes I'm entirely positive that I do, but we both have stuff we need to work out."

When she pulled away, Shane saw the fever in her eyes had calmed. Maybe Sarah's black tourmaline was already working.

"I'm going to go back in there and order another hot chocolate," Margaret said, pointing to Ram's Horn's back door.

"I'm going to get in this car, drive to my apartment, and go to sleep," he answered, pointing to the Cavalier.

"See. We're already working it out."

§

A few days later, after lights out and when Shane usually took his lunch, he and Mrs. Michaels were outside, on the far side of the Medicomplex where the glare of the yellow security lights wouldn't find them. Shane knew he would have to sneak away later during his shift, to scarf down a bologna sandwich and a package of chocolate Teddy Grahams, his reward for having endured another three-hour, guilt-laced dinner with his folks.

It was cold enough for Shane to see his breath mingling with the marijuana smoke in the fading light. He was already worried about what they would do when winter came and Mrs. Michaels had to toke in the snow.

"Do you have boots?" Shane asked.

Mrs. Michaels politely handed Shane the joint, but he just held it until she was ready to smoke again, unwilling to get high on the job now that he was the night shift supervisor.

Her face was mostly obscured by shadow but he could still see her smile. "You worry too much, Sal Paradise," she said.

"Worrying about you is my job."

"Did you ever think that I might not live long enough to need boots?"

He had, and the thought filled his stomach with a dread that he could not name. "Don't say that."

"People refrain from talking about death because they're afraid of it, but I'm not afraid."

"Is that because you'll get to see your Raymond again?"

She seemed to think for a moment before responding. "That's a nice thought, isn't it? But that isn't why. Why would I be afraid to die when I was never afraid to live?"

When Mrs. Michaels took back the joint and inhaled, the end illuminated her quiet face like a smoldering coal, as red and deep as a gem.

The Disenchanted Youth

During the summer, there was hardly a distinction between the lunch rush and dinner rush—the Speiselokal dining rooms teamed with tourists: fathers in pleat-front khakis belted below their waists; mothers in Sketchers tennis shoes preparing for or recovering from a day of outlet mall shopping; kids picking at their dinners, anticipating the soft-serve ice cream that came with the All You Care To Eat Chicken Feast. It was a steady stream of hungry out-of-towners reeking of Hawaiian Tropics sunscreen, willing to sit in the over-air conditioned anteroom, sometimes for hours, for the pleasure of being served dark beer by a guy in lederhosen. Whole families stood, necks craned and eyes shaded from the sun, to watch the famous Speiselokal glockenspiel play out the story of the Pied Piper of Hamlin. The garishly painted wooden figures from the legend tracked in and out of mechanical doors, while the story droned in German through a loudspeaker at noon, three, and six.

But by the end of August, the river of tourists had receded. When I entered the Literatur Dining Room for my luncheon shift, only a few tables were occupied—snowy-haired retirees on fixed incomes that would, undoubtedly, try to use expired circular coupons to haggle over every penny of their bill.

In the kitchen, I tried using my distorted reflection in the stainless industrial refrigerator to pin my red and white flower crown in place.

"You're crooked," Pam said, setting her tray on the counter next to the coffee maker. Predictably, her tray was laden with bread and a pot of hot water for tea, because old people have to drink hot tea, even when it's eighty degrees outside.

It was early—Pam smelled like lavender talcum powder and cigarette smoke as she straightened the crown on my head, pinned it in place, and parted the dangling ribbons around my ponytail. By the end of the shift, we would both smell, inescapably, like fried chicken.

"Thanks," I said, and followed her out into the dining room. I watched as she explained to her table how "stollen is a traditional German dried fruit bread," how "we make the strawberry jam fresh on the premises," how "the rye bread is a traditional recipe brought to the United States in 1904 by Anna Herzog, matriarch of the Speiselokal founding family." There was no hint in Pam's delivery that she'd been saying the same speech for almost thirty years, that she probably helped my mother with her flower crown when Mom still worked in the dining room, that she'd be saying the same speech until she was old enough to retire. That was just how Königshofen worked—you got out while you were young or you stayed for life.

"You got sat," Pam said on her way back to the kitchen.

I watched Sherry, the hostess, place menus in the blue-veined hands of an elderly couple, heard her say, "Your server, Carrie, will be with you shortly."

By the time I reached the table, the woman had already unearthed her circular coupons from her pocketbook.

"We would like to share the All You Care to Eat Chicken Feast, dear. And I would also like a pot of hot tea."

I knew two things without looking: the coupons were expired

and it was going to be a long day.

§

When I started at Speiselokal right after graduation, I knew I'd be driven to madness, I just didn't know if it'd be by the itchy seams in my red and white polyester milkmaid serving costume or by the never ending German polkas piped throughout the restaurant. But after working there all summer, I had built up a tolerance for both, and was just thankful that I'd gotten a job at the restaurant instead of at the Nativity Museum gift shop like my best friend Gretchen. She hadn't really talked about it all summer, but I figured eventually she would hear Dean Martin's "Walkin' in a Winter Wonderland" one too many times and start stabbing tourists with imported blown-glass wise men. Luckily for her, she left for college before that happened.

I hadn't seen Gretchen since the middle of August, when she packed up her parents' Ford Explorer with clothes, a mini fridge, and the quilt her grandmother made for her, and moved to Grand Rapids. While I was serving dressing with chicken gravy to retirees, she was eating Easy Mac and attending Grand Valley State University Week of Welcome events.

Gretchen's dad was the only dentist in Königshofen—he had seen inside the mouths of every one of its residents and could afford Grand Valley's $20,000 a year in tuition and fees. My mother, former Speiselokal waitress and current bookkeeper, could not.

At the start of my senior year, when it became clear that no long lost relative would oblige us by dying and leaving me a college-sustaining fortune, Mom and I struck a deal.

I was sitting at the kitchen table, my Pre-Calc textbook open to Inverse Functions. Mom had her back to me, heating milk on the stove for hot cocoa. Without turning, she said, "I know you're disappointed that I can't just pay for your college like Gretchen's folks."

I put my pencil down but said nothing—I was disappointed, and

Mom and I had been friends for too long for me to lie about it.

I watched as she took the milk off the heat and stirred in the chocolate powder, then poured the mixture into mugs. Mine said "It's Always Christmas in Königshofen," with a fading picture of the Nativity Scene Museum beneath it.

"Here's the thing—no matter what, we're both going to have to take on debt for your school. I hate the idea of you having to mortgage your future, not least of all because a degree isn't worth what it once was."

"But, Mom, at least it's a shot. I'll be serving chicken forever if I don't go to school."

"Not necessarily," Mom said and sipped her cocoa. "If you're very good at your job you could be promoted to bookkeeper."

Her tone was light, but I knew these conversations hurt her feelings, that I might as well just say, "I need to go to college so I can do more with my life than you."

"So here's my plan—after graduation, you get a job in town—the restaurant, one of the shops, the hotel, anywhere. For two years, you can work and save, and I can help you pay to get some of your prerequisite classes out of the way at Delta. That way, you won't be starting that far behind the other kids in your graduating class."

"And after two years, I can go to Grand Valley?" I asked, cocoa forgotten.

"If that's what you want."

It was what I wanted, and the day after graduation, I started at Speiselokal full time and enrolled in Fundamentals in Oral Communication, as part of Delta College's Associates in Accounting degree. It was a lot—compared to Gretchen, who only worked a couple shifts at the museum each week in order to have spending money during the school year. I never had any down time. But there are three kinds of graduates from Königshofen High School—the Leavers, like Gretchen, who go to college and get out; the Lifers, like my mom, who get townie jobs and stay; and the Burnouts who do neither. They get jobs at the outlet mall, the gas station, or the fast food joints just outside of town, before falling off the grid all together. I knew which one I wanted to be.

§

Toward the end of my shift, the busboy called in sick, and Mr. Herzog asked if I would please bus tables to help prepare for the dinner rush. He was manager of Speiselokal and my boss, but he never let anyone forget that he was the great-grandson of Wilhelm Herzog, one of the cofounders of Königshofen.

"What dinner rush?" I muttered to the back of Mr. Herzog's head, which was balding despite his spectacular grey mustache.

The dining room was about half full, and I wondered, as I piled dirty dishes onto my tray, if they would even need to open the Lied dining room for dinner, which was larger and had murals of famous German composers on the wall. During the summer, all three dining rooms—Literatur, Lied, and Kunst, the smallest and most elegant with crystal chandeliers and framed reproductions of famous German paintings on the wall—were used all day long. I thought the Literatur was the ugliest of the three, with murals of German authors and depictions of famous scenes from their works staring at diners as they ate. The Brothers Grimm wall, with scenes from "Snow White" and "Hansel and Gretel," wasn't so bad, but I was clearing the corner booth, where a mural of Goethe seemed to watch nervously as a bat-winged Mephistopheles made a pact with knowledge-seeking Faust. Who would want to eat next to that?

I finally escaped a half hour later, sweaty and irritated. I'd accidentally bumped a table on the way to the kitchen with my last load of dishes and upset an almost-full boat of congealed chicken gravy, spilling most of it down my front.

"And we're done!" I said, slamming the tray of dishes on the counter next to the giant sink. The dishwasher, a fifteen-year-old named Brad, his liberal smattering of acne bright red from the heat and moisture belching from the industrial dishwasher, took one look at the translucent ring of grease spreading out from the brown stain on my apron and started snickering.

"Laugh it up," I said, ripping the flower crown off my head and stomping out the back door toward the dumpsters and, beyond that, the employee parking lot.

"Where's the fire, Fraulein?"

I turned, ready to tell Brad to fuck off, but instead saw Tobias, one of the dinner waiters. I knew him from high school. He'd graduated two years ahead of me, but I'd never worked with him.

Tobias, finishing a cigarette before his shift, wore the gray suede lederhosen, white tasseled knee socks, and green felt hat with requisite feather glued to the side that was the men's serving costume. They had it worse than the women, even with the flower crowns. The Marlboro pinched between his thumb and index finger looked incongruous.

"I'm going home." I displayed my newly-acquired gravy stain.

"Long shift?" he asked. I felt more kindly towards him when he grimaced sympathetically.

"You can bet your ass it was, and my tips were a joke."

"You should talk to Herzog about transferring to nights," Tobias said. "Tips aren't great in the off season, but they're way better than working swing shifts for pennies. There should be some openings— Oktoberfest is coming and we lost a bunch of servers to college."

Whatever meaning it had in Germany, Oktoberfest in Königshofen was when frat guys from Central and Kettering filled the town at the end of September and drank their weights in beer. Last year, Gretchen and I hung around outside the restaurant to check them out, figuring college guys would have to be better than the Lifers and Burnouts KHS routinely produced. Two douchey drunk guys, wearing boat shoes without socks and skinny jeans, tried to pick us up. One, with his blazer sleeves rolled to the elbows, turned a bleary eye on me and told me I looked "sexy." He seriously said "sexy." Gretchen and I laughed in his face, drove to the Dairy Queen north of town, and discussed how tourists are the lowest common denominator of human being. The soft serve with peanuts and hot fudge helped ease the sting of disappointment.

Tobias took a final drag off his cigarette, ground the butt under his toe, and yanked the kitchen door open to go inside.

"Thanks for the tip," I said to his back. "Have a good shift."

He turned, said, "Better than yours, I hope," and let the door slam shut behind him.

§

When I got home, my mother was eating Stouffer's lasagna in front of the TV, engrossed in a *Law and Order* rerun, a half drunk glass of milk next to her feet on the coffee table.

"You're home late," she said, pausing the show.

When I walked into the living room, she gasped.

"Nice, huh? The stupid busser called off, so Herzog had me cleaning tables."

"MISTER Herzog. And it's just gravy." Mom followed me into my room. "Get your uniform off—the sooner we treat it, the easier it will come out."

"Think you could talk MISTER Herzog into giving me a couple night shifts?" I asked. Mom unzipped my dress.

"I thought the restaurant would take over your life if you worked nights."

"Yeah, well, I made shit for tips today." The t-shirt I grabbed from my pajama drawer was an old one of hers, soft from years of washing, with a faded picture of the Speiselokal glockenspiel and the words "Königshofen, Michigan's Little Germany," rainbowed over it. "The only reason today wasn't a total bust was because of a townie office party that came in right before my shift ended. It should have been Pam's table, but she let me take it."

"Pam's good people," Mom said, scraping at the gravy stain with a butter knife.

"I agree, but I am not stupid enough to expect charity every day."

"Pam's got your back—she knows why you're working so hard. Why can't you ask Mr. Herzog yourself?"

I wrinkled my nose at her. "Because he likes you, Mom."

"Oh!" Mom left my uniform draped over the bathroom sink and returned with dish soap, which she massaged into the stain with warm water. "Now you're being silly."

But I wasn't being silly, and she knew it—everyone did! Mr. Herzog had a crush on my mother, despite the fact that he was fifteen years older than she, at least.

"Please?"

Mom heaved a sigh, dumped my serving costume in the washing machine with a capful of Cheer, and closed the washer lid before saying, "Okay. I'll ask when I go in tomorrow."

I hugged her and went into the kitchen to help myself to some lasagna.

"What's on the agenda for tonight?" Mom asked.

I carried my dish of lasagna and a tangerine Diet Rite into the living room and took a seat next to her on the couch. Even with the bathroom door closed, the walls of our tiny apartment were paper thin, and the sound of my serving uniform in the washing machine was as loud as the restaurant dishwasher, sans pimply operator.

"I'm starting a class terrifyingly called Principles of Macroeconomics. I have to read chapters one and two and answer some discussion questions online before Friday." My lasagna was cold, but I was too tired to get up and microwave it. The Diet Rite was also cold, but it was supposed to be.

"Have you heard from Gretchen?"

"Not for two weeks, when she texted me photos of her dorm room and Nancy."

"Who's Nancy?"

"Her Chicago roommate. What kind of name is Nancy, anyway?" I asked.

"Maybe she's a teenage detective?" Mom offered.

"What?"

"Didn't you read Nancy Drew when you were younger? I kept all of my books."

"*Babysitters Club.* Anyway, maybe I'll try texting her before I start my homework. I'm still planning to visit her in a week or so, assuming she hasn't forgotten me."

"I'm sure she's just busy settling in. You've been busy, too." When I shrugged, Mom started the TV going, but then paused it again to ask, "Do you want me to rewind this *Law and Order* to the beginning?"

"Nah—I can catch it when it plays again in a few months."

If I hadn't had a dish of lasagna in my hand, she would have lobbed a sofa pillow at me—nobody disses the *Law and Order* in OUR apartment. As it was, she just finished her glass of milk, instead.

§

By the next night, two things had been settled: Herzog posted the next week's schedule, with me moved to nights, and I'd arranged to visit Gretchen in a week.

When Gretchen finally emailed, she apologized for being an absentee friend, blamed her scattered brain on crummy dorm coffee and a class called "Oceanography—The Last Frontier," which was in actuality a class about silt and seafloor composition. Most of her email, however, agonized over Rich, a guy who played lacrosse, a sport I'd never heard of, who lived on her floor, and was, according to her, "too beautiful for words."

And if that wasn't enough of an enticement, I was absurdly

gratified that things with roommate Nancy weren't going well. Gretchen had taken to referring to her as "the one who snores," or t.o.w.s., for short. I think it was the chance to glower at t.o.w.s. while Gretch and I ate in the dining hall that inspired me to answer, "Yes, of course I'm still coming," as soon as I read her email.

§

I was happy to get more than six tables during my first evening shift, but what was really different was the feeling behind the scenes. After the summer craziness, it was like a hush had fallen over the kitchen during the day shift. The quasi-hibernation of a tourist town in the off-season. Most days, it was just Pam and me on the floor, working with a skeletal kitchen crew: the oldest cooks; Marta, who only spoke German and made all of our bread; and one of the dishwashers. Lifers and Future-Lifers sleepwalking through our shifts.

While the kitchen wasn't crazy like the restaurant in summer, the staff just seemed more alive at night—a cohesive unit attuned to the ebb and flow of the dinner crowd. As I rushed to place orders and deliver food to the table, I caught snippets of inside jokes, of references to regular customers both present and absent in the dining room. And even though the majority of the night staff was either my age or a little older, I felt set adrift. I'd had a role to play when I worked days—I was Amanda's daughter, the "young one" with big ambitions. I'd been afforded certain privileges and considerations, like when Pam let me have the office party table.

It was weird to suddenly be no one.

My final table of the night was a group of bikers from Bay City passing through on their way to the "hearse show" in Hell, Michigan. One offered, in a good-natured way, to let me ride bitch if I wanted to go. I told him, demurely, that road dust would stain my uniform and hoped for a big tip.

The bikers ordered the All You Care to Eat Chicken Feast with two additional meats—my tray was loaded with a platter of chicken, a platter of bratwurst, a plate of pork schnitzel with mushroom gravy on the side, mashed potatoes, and a bowl of spaetzle. I knelt to get under the tray in order to lift it with my legs, but before I could try, I heard, "Need some help, Fraulein?"

When I turned, I saw Tobias eyeing my tray. Not to be outdone, I tried to stand—but couldn't.

"Schnitzel is heavier than it looks," he said.

"I built up some freakish upper-body strength over the summer, but I guess this was too ambitious. I can just make two trips."

I went to remove the platter of bratwurst from the tray, but Tobias said, "Let me at least try to lift it, first. My final table is lingering over coffee, anyway."

Tobias was just barely able to lift the tray—his face going red and veins sticking out of his neck with the strain. I cleared the way for him and opened the tray stand. He didn't even upset the gravy, and the bikers, foam crusting the inside of their empty beer glasses, cheered. If Tobias had been trying to impress me, it kinda worked.

Despite the fact that their voracious appetites kept me running to and from the kitchen, the bikers were the best table I'd had in weeks, and they were generous tippers. I was exhausted but pleased as I helped the busboy clear the rest of the dishes. Tobias came into the dining room from the back holding a hoky and started sweeping around the bikers' table.

"How'd it go?" he asked.

"Good. It's not summer tips, but it's better than working the day shift."

"Told you."

I followed Tobias into the kitchen. The dishwasher, a high schooler I didn't recognize, was taking the last load of dishes from the sanitizer, while Jesse, one of the night shift cooks, wiped down the stainless steel countertops.

"Big plans tonight?" Tobias asked.

"Huge. A whole chapter of macroeconomics is waiting up for me."

Tobias made a face. "Homework's for Sundays. You should come out with us."

"Us?"

"My band's playing and a bunch of the guys from work are gonna come see it."

"I didn't know you had a band," I said, zipping my sweatshirt up over my costume.

"Most people don't, and it's too bad. It's one of my more charming attributes."

"Well, where are you playing?" I asked, refusing to smile.

"The Dive."

The Dive used to be a fancy microbrewery in the no man's land between downtown and the outlet malls—not close enough to the hotel and restaurant to get overflow tourist traffic, and too far from the stores to coax the day trippers from their shopping and Sbarros. It went belly up when I was in middle school, and has since become a haven for Lifers and Burnouts. Gretchen and I went once—we paid five bucks at the door to watch a shitty My Chemical Romance cover band and drink flat Pepsi.

But my alternative was macroeconomics.

"Sure," I said. "I'll go."

§

I grudgingly parted with five dollars at the door and was gratified when I saw the bouncer sniff the bill before adding it to the stack—my tips smelled like chicken.

It was murky inside The Dive—many of the hipstery track lighting fixtures had gone out, and the bulbs that were left created uneven light pools that seemed to accentuate the darkness between.

In the sea of t-shirts and jeans, it wasn't hard to spot the other Speiselokal refugees—hooded sweatshirts and jackets doing little to mute the garish red and blue of the milkmaid costumes, the white knee socks of the men in lederhosen. I was thankful I'd remembered to shed my flower crown in the car, but the other members of the wait staff made me feel less conspicuous.

As I approached the group, I heard one of the waitresses say, "Tobias even conned the new kid into seeing his band play." Then she turned to me and said, "Greetings, new kid."

"Hey," I replied. I knew her name was Samantha—she graduated two years before I did, and maybe it was this age gap, or else she was too steeped in her existence as a Lifer to remember high school, but she gave no indication of knowing me. I felt like I was playing a game where I didn't know the rules, so I followed her lead and pretended to be a stranger.

"You a big fan of Oompop?" Samantha asked me.

"I don't know what that is."

She gave a short laugh and grinned—not in a friendly way. "Guess you'll find out."

The stage at The Dive was just a platform erected where the giant metal microbrew tanks used to be, crisscrossed with extension cords and power strips, with one lone folding chair off to the side. Three microphones, which looked, even from twenty feet away, like they had seen better days, were set in stands. The stage was illuminated by theater lights on metal trees that got so hot they'd make you sweat if you stood too close.

Without any introduction or fanfare, Tobias and the other members of his band walked out on the stage from a backroom, each carrying their own instruments. It was clear that this was not going to be a repeat of the My Chemical Romance cover band—Tobias had an oboe. Another guy I didn't recognize, but who looked a bit older, had a trombone; a short girl who looked like she was in middle school had the smallest accordion in the world strapped to her chest; and the final member, another girl who looked my age but sported bright pink hair, was carrying a cello.

The girl with pink hair, whose long black skirt matched her cello and purple camo tank top matched her hair, walked to the center microphone, "Thanks for coming out to hear us. We're Vertrocknet. I'm Sarah on cello. Tobias is on oboe." Tobias was still wearing the Speiselokal lederhosen, but he had shed his white collar shirt and tie in favor of an old t-shirt that faintly read "Königshofen: Follow the Beer." He blew into the oboe and made it squeak. "Mindy's on concertina." Mindy squeezed the accordion and it sighed impatiently. "And Dan's on trombone." Instead of playing a note, Dan just held his instrument aloft, and a girl in the audience squealed.

I understood the need for Sarah with the pink hair's long skirt— she took a seat in the folding chair and placed the cello between her legs. When the band started to play, I thought at first it was just a regular polka—like all the rest of the polkas I listen to every day at work. But when they got to the refrain, the melody was familiar, and not in the "I don't want her you can have her she's too fat for me" way. Tobias played the oboe in place of a singer, so it took me longer to realize that they were playing a strange, polka-ed version of "The Freshman" by The Verve Pipe.

I turned to Samantha standing next to me. With the trombone playing, the music was too loud to speak over, but she mouthed "Oompop," or maybe she mouthed "Fuck off," either way, her smile seemed more genuine, so I smiled back.

I didn't recognize all of the songs Vertrocknet played. One in the middle might have been "Radioactive" by Imagine Dragons, but it was hard to tell without the heavy base line. The final song of their set was easy to recognize because Mindy sang the lyrics while she played her tiny accordion. Mindy's voice was strong despite her tiny stature, and she did justice to Candlebox's "Far Behind."

While the music played, bottles of beer had appeared in the hands of the Speiselokal crew, and once the band was finished, I debated between getting myself a soda or just leaving. The rest of the wait staff were standing around talking, and while I wasn't exactly ignored, I wasn't a part of the conversation, either. Leaving had just about won out when Tobias appeared from a backroom, this time without his oboe, and joined the group.

He was clapped on the back, complimented on the new song arrangements, then he turned to me and asked, "You wanna beer, Fraulein?"

"I'm only nineteen."

"So, you wanna beer?"

"Okay."

I followed him as he wove his way through the crowd to the bar, its fancy copper surface was sticky and dented, almost completely oxidized from lack of maintenance. When Tobias ordered two beers, no one asked to see his ID.

"The DJ is setting up and it's gonna get loud in a sec. We can take these out back."

Tobias pointed to a door that led "backstage." I didn't know why we were ditching his friends, but he was cute, so I nodded and followed. Besides, the DJ was a scrawny guy I didn't recognize, the portrait of Elvis on his black tank top was done completely in glitter, which matched a glittering septum piercing. I didn't know what kind of music Glitter Elvis would be spinning, but I was almost positive it would be more than I wanted to take on top of an already long evening.

"Out back" was just that—The Dive's back alley. We sat on concrete steps close to the dumpster, but The Dive didn't serve food and it only smelled like stale beer and rusting metal. Had we been this close to the Speiselokal dumpster, not even the cold would have been able to keep the rotting-chicken-carcass stench from being gag-inducing.

"So, what'd you think?" Tobias asked.

I took a drink of my beer, a Coors Light that tasted like fizzy water but at least was cold enough to make my teeth ache.

"Your music was interesting," I finally said.

I thought I'd chosen my words carefully, but he responded with, "That bad?"

"Not bad—but weird. Very very weird. A polka version of 'The Freshman'?"

My honest response seemed to satisfy him, because he laughed and said, "Yeah, well, that's all Sarah. She loves 90s alternative music."

"So Sarah's the leader?"

"She's a classically trained cellist and adapts all the songs for the band," Tobias said. "I know her from KHS. Dan, too. He and I were in the band but he graduated my freshman year."

"No offense, but if Sarah's so good, what's she doing here?" When I heard classically trained cellist, I imagined concert halls in New York, or at the very least, first chair with the Detroit Symphony Orchestra. "Vertrocknet" was a far cry from even Königshofen's community orchestra, which sometimes played concerts in the hotel's ballroom.

Tobias offered no more explanation than to say, "She's doing what she wants to do."

"Ah."

"So, what's the homework you're blowing off to see my band?"

"Macroeconomics. I'm taking classes at Delta until I can transfer to Grand Valley."

"So, are you going to be a macroeconomist?" Tobias asked, his tongue tripping over his joke.

"I don't think that's a thing," I said and laughed. "It's a class I have to take to be an accountant."

"Is it fun?"

I thought about last week's chapter, covering a concept called

Specialization that I'd had a hard time wrapping my head around. On the discussion board, we had to give an example of a real life business that epitomized the concept. I picked the Speiselokal, and had been lambasted by my classmates in the comments. I realized my mistake—but it wasn't "fun." Frustrating and embarrassing, maybe. Tobias's question was stupid and I felt annoyed when I replied.

"Well, it's hard," I said. "But that's why they call it work. If it was fun, they wouldn't pay people to do it."

The music started up inside—I could hear the pulsing beat coming faintly through the building's brick walls, imagined that same beat throbbing the inside of my skull if I was still standing next to the night servers. Even though the night was almost too cold for sitting on a concrete step in the dark, I was glad to be out there.

"I'm not convinced that a job needs to be all work and no play," Tobais said. "I think Speiselokal is pretty fun."

"You're joking. You like this?" I grabbed one of his suspenders, printed with flowers and made of the ever-so-traditional elastic, and snapped it. "I don't want to be a Lifer in a tourist trap, serving chicken to bitter retirees and fat families, wearing a milkmaid's outfit until I die."

"Stop sugar coating it. Tell me how you really feel."

I knew it was just a thing you say, but Tobias settled back against the cast iron railing, as if waiting to hear how I really felt. And I wanted to tell him, because he wasn't my mother and I didn't care if I hurt his feelings. Because, if I hurt his feelings, he was still young enough to make a different choice and be a Leaver.

"I just don't get the appeal. I've waited on people from all over the state. Folks drive down from the U.P. I've waited on folks from Illinois and Ohio. I had a Canadian table over the summer. For chicken. They drive hundreds of miles to be fed chicken by me, no more German than 'The Freshman,' and to look at creepy nativity scenes at the museum when it's not even Christmas."

I could feel my heart pounding and when I took a drink of my beer, my hand was shaking.

"Feel better?" Tobias asked.

I nodded.

"Then I'll tell you, I think you have it wrong with your tourist trap scenario."

"How so?"

"We're not the world's largest ball of twine, Carrie. Königshofen's a real thing—the Herzogs and a handful of other families moved here from Germany in the 1800s and started the town."

"Yeah, okay. But do you think my Bay City bikers know or care about that?"

"You said you didn't get the appeal. I'm telling you what it is. Even if they don't know the history, this is why people come. It's dressed up in chicken and schnitzel and German beer and polka, but people come to feel a part of something bigger, to be included in a history and a culture for a short time."

I shook my head.

"So you're not German, but a lot of Königshofen still is. Our entire band is. Dan's been playing the trombone since he was eleven years old, and he played in a Kinder Polka band until he started high school. Mindy's concertina belonged to her grandmother, who smuggled it from Germany wrapped in underwear."

"And Sarah?" I asked. There was nothing traditional about magenta hair.

"She's the Germanest of all. She first learned about oompop when she lived in Germany for a year, playing with the Bavarian State Orchestra. She knew a lot of people like her back home, who'd been playing polka since they were little, and figured this would be a good way of putting all that training to use."

"And this is enough for you? Lederhosen, 'The Freshman,' and

Herzog's mustache?"

"It is what it is. Today, I wear suede pants to serve chicken or play the oboe in a rock band, and I'm okay with it."

I didn't know how, but I knew I'd made a mistake. Somehow, the whole conversation had gone off track. At that point, Tobias should have realized that we are all part of an elaborate money-making scheme, and that to stay—in Königshofen, at Speiselokal— was to give up.

I stood and stretched my legs, tossed my empty beer bottle into the dumpster, where the crash of glass against metal reverberated off the walls of the alley, satisfyingly punctuating our conversation.

"I better go," I said. "Thanks for the beer."

"Wait," he grabbed my sleeve. "You're mad."

"No," I said. "Just—frustrated. We're speaking different languages. I feel like I tried to explain something important to you, but you didn't understand."

He sighed, and I wondered if I was frustrating him, too. It had been a weird night.

"Well, have you ever stopped to watch the glockenspiel?" he finally asked. It wasn't the response I was expecting.

"What?"

"I'm serious. Have you ever stopped and really looked at it? The figures were hand carved and painted in Germany, and the Herzogs brought the parts and the artisans over in the 1960s so it could be constructed in Königshofen."

"I've read the plaque out in front of the restaurant, too," I snapped. "If you haven't noticed, when the glockenspiel plays, the story's told in German, which I don't speak."

"But you know the story of the Pied Piper, right? I mean, you don't really need to understand the words in order to watch it and know what's going on."

I didn't want to be having this conversation anymore—I wanted to go home, to count my tips and remind myself that this night wasn't a total bust. "I guess not," I said.

"Well, you should."

"Okay, sure. I will."

Tobias let go of my sleeve and I walked from the back alley to the parking lot and my car, glad that I didn't need to go back inside The Dive to escape.

§

I sat across from Gretchen in the Commons, one of GVSU's dining halls, which was really more like the food court at the outlet mall, eating a teriyaki chicken sandwich from Subway. When I expressed my disappointment at not having a more "traditional" dining hall experience, with plastic trays and indiscernible casseroles steaming in the hot food line, Gretchen scoffed, said, "You've seen too many college movies."

Gretchen was wearing a heather grey GVSU t-shirt, which she "got for free when she opened a checking account at the credit union." Her hair was shorter than I had ever seen it, a cap of strawberry blonde curls that was "easier to deal with when I'm too busy to shower."

"So, your room's pretty nice," I said. It was a one hundred and fifty square foot box containing lofted beds with desks beneath. I knew Gretchen's bed because of her quilt from home—she also had a brand new laptop, a poster of Damon from the *Vampire Diaries* show, and a stack of blu-ray discs piled next to her combination television/blu-ray disc player. *Pitch Perfect*, which we'd seen seven times in the theatre, was at the bottom of the pile.

"I guess it's okay—when t.o.w.s. isn't there, anyway. She's home this weekend, by the way. I am almost one hundred percent sure she left because you were coming. Whatever—that means you can stay in her bed."

"She won't mind?"

"She won't know."

"Well, when I transfer in two years, maybe you and I can get a room together," I said.

"An apartment, anyway. Only freshman live in dorm housing."

Disappointment rose like a bitter wave up my throat. I took several sips from my Dr. Pepper to choke it back down, telling myself that an apartment would be just as good.

Gretchen didn't notice, and continued, "It's so cool that you were able to come tonight. I didn't know Rich's band was going to be playing until a few days ago. It'll be awesome to take you to a real event."

"What kind of music does Rich's band play?" I asked.

"I know they covered some Beck. Maybe the Flaming Lips? Not sure, but they're good."

"Have you ever heard of oompop?"

"Is that the new Starbucks soda, 'cause I tried the root beer, and it wasn't that great." Gretchen pulled her phone from her back pocket and considered it. "Well, we've got an hour or so before the show starts. I can walk you through the center of campus if you'd like to see where I have my classes."

§

I drove Gretchen and me to a coffee shop just off campus, called The Art House. Gretchen explained that before it served coffee, The Art House had been an actual tiny house built in the 1800s, when Allendale was first being settled. The art pieces hanging on the walls, everything from paintings to a collage that looked like water bottles all melted together, were created by GVSU students and for sale.

I regarded the painting nearest to the line while Gretchen and I waited to order coffee—it was a sea of red with what looked like pictures of arms and legs clipped from magazines glued throughout. According to the information card, it was called "Skin Deep," and the aspiring artist thought it was worth $200. In her dreams.

A dirty chintz couch with sagging cushions was crammed with bodies, as were the rickety two-top tables scattered throughout what had once been the ground floor of the house. Gretch and I ultimately found a place to stand and drink our $5 vanilla lattes, next to an old brick fireplace that must have once been used to heat the home, but now was painted a glossy black and filled with flickering candles at various stages of use.

There was no stage—just a couple of amplifiers set up in a corner. When the "band" arrived, it was two guys carrying hard-side guitar cases, and one guy carrying what looked like a suitcase covered in switches and dials.

"What's that thing?" I asked Gretchen.

"A drum machine. When they play a small venue like this one, Jimmy can't fit a full on drum kit in here, so he uses the machine. I told you they're good—they take their music very seriously. One of those things costs thousands of dollars."

I didn't understand how dropping a wad of cash on an electronic toy equated to a seriousness about music, but I decided not to press it. What I did understand is that the band looked like an ad for Abercrombie and Fitch—skinny jeans rolled at the ankles, polo shirts with popped collars, Jimmy-the-drummer was even wearing flip flops—in Michigan, in September. It was as if the catalog photographer had said, "Here, take these instruments and pretend to be in a garage band."

I wanted to share my impressions with Gretchen, but she seemed too busy trying to catch Rich's eye so she could wave to him from the audience, to laugh at my hilarious commentary.

I assumed that one of the hard side guitar cases would be a base, but no—both Rich and the other band member not Jimmy played guitar. Instead of introducing themselves, Rich just said, "One two three," and the band launched into Beck's "Loser." There was a cheer from the audience, and Gretchen set her coffee on the fireplace mantle to join, but the clapping couldn't drown out the music—the amps were turned up too loud, and I could feel a headache starting, radiating in from my eardrums. The only part of the song that sounded remotely like Beck was the drumming, or the part that was being reproduced via machine.

I lasted two more songs—a decent "Buddy Holly" by Weezer and a version of The Postal Service's "The District Sleeps Alone Tonight" that was so bad, I was pushed over the edge.

I pulled my phone out of my pocket as if I felt it going off, mouthed to Gretchen, "One minute," and went outside to take a call that hadn't come.

For being a house that was built in the 1800s, it did a good job of keeping the noise inside, and I was able to take a breath and think. I stepped off the dark porch onto the sidewalk, which was illuminated by security lights.

I didn't know what my problem was—other than, from the moment I arrived, I felt like the tourist in Gretchen's life. I had wanted this time with her to be my positive reinforcement—that, if I slogged diligently through my accounting classes at Delta, in two years she and I would be able to pick up right where we left off. I would be welcomed into the magical fold that is college life.

Instead, I felt less sure than I'd ever been. Was this even what I wanted to do? Could I take it on faith that I would feel differently once I was a student here? I felt sick to my stomach and tossed the rest of my over-priced latte into a nearby trashcan.

The door of The Art House opened, and Gretchen stepped out onto the porch.

"Everything all right?" she asked from the dark.

"It was my mom," I lied. "Herzog needs me to cover an earlier shift tomorrow, so I gotta go."

"Really?" When she stepped off the porch to join me on the sidewalk, she at least looked genuinely disappointed, and guilt joined the uncomfortable party in my stomach. I nodded.

"Jeez, it's not like working the restaurant is your life, you know? They should give you a break."

"Do you need me to take you back to your dorm?" I asked, remembering that I'd driven us.

"No, I can catch a ride with Rich. But do you need anything out of my room?"

"My bag's in my car," I said. I hadn't even moved in that much.

"Okay. Well, I should be home in a few weeks. And maybe you can plan to come out for Halloween or something? I hear a lot of people throw parties and it's really fun."

"Sounds good."

Gretchen hugged me. In the harsh security light, her short hair looked almost white, her eyes shadowed in their sockets. I realized that she must use a different detergent here than she did at home—she didn't even smell familiar.

"You're sure you can't stay?"

"Positive," I said, this time with complete sincerity.

I watched as she climbed The Art House steps, disappearing in the porch darkness before opening the door. In a brilliant flash, she was illuminated, a portal of light and sound spilling from within, before the door closed behind her, leaving me in silence once more.

§

I am twenty minutes early for my shift.

Last night, I got back to town from GVSU at 2 a.m. and felt wired, whether from the vanilla latte or something else, I didn't know. I drove past The Dive, in the off-chance that Vertrocknet would be playing again, but the weedy parking lot was empty, the windows dark and deserted. I thrashed around in bed all night, woke late and unrested, and didn't feel up to tackling "Elasticity and Its Applications" before the dinner shift.

The glockenspiel is playing for the three o'clock show—I can hear the gravelly German words coming through the loudspeaker, rattling off the story of The Pied Piper, even from the back of the restaurant.

I'm early anyway, and thinking about Tobias's weird parting request, I take the long way around the building to watch the glockenspiel play. There's only a small crowd gathered beneath the tower, a father with his daughter sitting on his shoulders, an elderly couple holding hands. I watch with them as the wooden Pied Piper frees the folks of Hamlin from their plague of vermin, watch as the Mayor refuses to pay the Piper's fee of one thousand guilders, watch as the Piper exacts his revenge by luring the children of the town away with his magical pipe.

In the Speiselokal version of the story, there are two children who are left behind—one with a cloth painted over his eyes to denote blindness, one carved with a crutch to denote lameness. The Piper and the other children of the town disappear through a door that closes with a snap, and the two remaining children are forced to retreat the way they came. For the first time, I wish that I could understand German—were the children angry at being left behind? Were they ultimately thankful, when it became clear that their friends would never return?

Long after the tourists have filed into the restaurant, to their chicken and beer and hot tea, I stand under the clock, staring at the closed door behind which the Piper and the children disappeared. Tobias's words, about feeling a part of something bigger, are like a riddle waiting to be solved. If only I can figure out what the words mean.

ACKNOWLEDGEMENTS

"I Don't Belong Here" was previously published in *Coe Review 45:2.*

"The Makeshift Carrier" was previously published in *The Magnolia Review 1:2*

ABOUT THE AUTHOR

Christine M. Lasek spent the first 30 years of her life living in southeast Michigan. She holds a BA in English from the University of Michigan and an MFA in Fiction from the University of South Florida. Christine currently lives in Athens, Georgia, where she teaches creative writing and serves as the Academic Professional for the Creative Writing Program at the University of Georgia. Her work has appeared in print and online literary magazines. *Love Letters to Michigan* is her first short story collection. Find her online at www.christinemlasek.com